Wakefield Press

INNOCENT MURDER

Steve J. Spears has worked as a writer/actor/singer in film, TV, radio, stage and rock for 30 years. If anybody knows showbiz people and how to bump them off, it's Spears. He lives by the sea in Aldinga Beach, South Australia, where he is working on further volumes of *The Pentangeli Papers*.

By the same author

Murder at The Fortnight
Murder by Manuscript

Innocent MURDER

STEVE J. SPEARS

Wakefield
Press

Wakefield Press
1 The Parade West
Kent Town
South Australia 5067
www.wakefieldpress.com.au

First published 2005
Copyright © Steve J. Spears, 2005

Cover illustration by Katharine Stafford
Cover designed by Dean Lahn
Text designed by Clinton Ellicott, Wakefield Press
Typeset by Ryan Paine, Wakefield Press
Printed and bound by Hyde Park Press

National Library of Australia
Cataloguing-in-publication entry

Spears, Steve J., 1951–   .
Innocent murder.

ISBN 1 86254 664 9.

1. Murder – Fiction. I. Title. (Series: Spears, Steve J., 1951–
Pentangeli papers; 3).

A823.3

Publication of this book was assisted by the Commonwealth Government through the Australia Council, its arts funding and advisory body.

To my beautiful baby sister,

Toni.

'Please, Red,' she said. 'Please don't kill me.
I'm innocent! Believe me! I'm absolutely innocent!'
'No one's *that* innocent, baby,' snarled Red.
He shot her twice to make sure.

'Murder, Baby' by Rodney Bain
Mean Streets Magazine, 1941

*

p. 233 'STELLA'
stella = stellar
Pho: 'cellar'

p. 127 'PENTANGELI'
pen – TAN! – geli
pen = when. tan = ban. geli = jelly
Pho: 'when – BAN! – jelly'

p. 121 'NG'
'Ping' minus 'p' + 'ing' minus 'i' = (p)(i)ng.
Pho: '(Pi)ng'.

Phonetic Pronunciation in Modern Crime (5th edition)
Colette Keen, Atlanta Press, 2005

CONTENTS

PART 1
JUDAS, JUDAS

Judas, Judas, there's his bed.
Kiss his feet, kiss his head.
I told the priests you'd introduce 'em.
Told the priests that you're a twosome.

Judas, Judas, flirty, flirty.
Thought the gig was only thirty.
I told the priests that you got plans.
Told the priests you want a grand.

'Judas'
© Angela Drumm, 1969

1.

SMOKIN' JOE

Chinatown section of Viceroy Valley, known now and forever as Vice Valley. The grey face, the red-tinged eyes, the air of utter weariness show the man to be a doper – in particular, an opium smoker. A Chinese chauvinist might applaud the doper's sense of history; no speed, cocaine or heroin for this loser. He will live and die by the original thing – the poison of his ancestors – chasing the Dragon. He might be 30 or 60. His head is shaved, his clothes as shapeless as his Fu Manchu scraggle. When he walks his feet insist that the ground is a few millimetres higher than it is, so he is continually near-stumbling on non-existent steps. This is his third attempt to get into Miss Bliss tonight. Each time two massive Chinese tuxedo-ed doormen gently stop him.

'Come on, Joe. It's after midnight. Why you wanna come into Bliss? You too stoned to fuck da girls and anyway dey too expensive.'

The second says, 'And by da way, no offence, Joe, you smell. Mr Ma, he like all da customers to be gentlemen.' Mr Ma is the owner of Miss Bliss. One of Ma's gang of underage Chinatown dealers has sold Joe today's supply of opium.

The doper mumbles at the doormen, angry at their lack of

respect. He thinks he's thundering righteous abuse at them, but he's already so stoned all that's coming out his mouth is a slurred mumbly loop of village-peasant Cantonese. Both doormen are second generation Australian – their Cantonese is serviceable but spiced with big-city slang and English. What they are hearing out of the man's mouth is the real pure thing.

'Jesus,' says Doorman #1, 'he sounds like he's right off da boat.'

Doorman #2 smiles affectionately. 'When he angry, he sound just like my grandfa'er used ta.'

The doormen have a soft spot for Joe – he's picked up the street name Smokin' Joe for his love of the opium pipe, and spends countless hours in the alley behind Miss Bliss in a stoned otherworld. He turned up about six weeks ago and seemed to take root there. At first the doormen would slap him round and send him on his way but the next day he'd be back. Smokin' Joe told them once when he was less blasted than usual that he liked to sit out in the alley on the steps because when the brothel door opened, the smell of powder and perfume reminded him of his wife, of his village Linlin, of China.

'She dead. She never leave my head.' Joe is a wrecked ruined poet.

A large black BMW pulls up outside. Mr Ma himself steps out with two bodyguards. He heads for the door, stops, peers at Joe.

'What's this bum doing here all the time?'

'Sorry Mr Ma. He from Linlin. We t'ought . . .'

'Linlin?'

'And da poor bastard wife's dead.'

Mr Ma was known as much for his great heart as for his great power. He speaks into the bum's face, but gentle. 'I came here from Linlin as a boy. My mother died young, maybe just like your wife.' He turns to the doormen. 'Let him be. He'll bring us luck. Give him fifty bucks.'

Joe thanks Mr Ma who nods and disappears inside. Joe starts to follow but the doormen gently push him back.

'Stay.'

'Good boy.'

'You a big man now, Joe. Mr Ma like you.'

'Smokin' Joe da man.'

Joe is about to continue arguing for his right to enter, then seems to forget about it. He turns and wanders off, high-stepping over invisible things. The doormen marvel at how he seems to have already forgotten the lovely girls inside and how much he wanted to see their bodies and smell them – forgotten the loneliness of a man far from home who's stripped himself of every grace and notion of honour. They figure, if he's thinking at all, he's wondering how he found himself in this cold city with a hopeless addiction – how he got so all alone.

He mumbles into the left lapel of his grubby suitcoat, 'Ng here. Did you hear that? Come in.'

A tiny female voice replies from the minuscule microphone/receiver under Joe's lapel, 'Got it. Come in.'

'Are we done? Come in.'

'We're done. Let's all go home and get some sleep. Come in.'

'Copy that. Out.'

*

The tiny room in Viceroy Valley's Famous Guest House has a single bed with sagging centre, a 60 watt globe, a table, a chair. The only luxury is an ancient tin food cupboard nailed high on the wall. Investigator Ng suspects that a previous guest hoped to make a home of this hovel, to the modest extent of keeping rats from his food.

5

But the rats found a way to get up the wall and attack the cupboard. Maybe they flew. Who knew? There are bite holes and teeth marks all through it. The rest is rust.

Tomorrow it begins again. Ng will swallow a tiny piece of saltpetre. Within minutes his face will turn grey and sickly. He'll carry a half lemon and dab it in his eyes. He'll buy a ball of opium from one of Mr Ma's underage runners, palm it and smoke the fake stuff in his other home – the alley behind Miss Bliss.

Tomorrow it begins again.

2.

CHAIN OF COMMAND

SHOWBIZ! SHOWBIZ! SHOWBIZ! ONLINE!
THE PENTANGELI PAPERS ***EXCLUSIVE***!
STRING'S THE THING
The Pentangeli Papers *hears from sources inside Channel 3*
that, since the arrival of Frank String in 3's supersoap
The Young and The Naked, *ratings have soared*
and morale onset has never been higher.
Frank String, of course, has been a star for over five decades
and is a true filmbiz legend.
He plays the conniving but loveable Harold Bellbird,
patriarch of the grazier Bellbird clan.
Mr String is said to be 'delighted to be part of Channel 3's
family' and 'an avid fan of TY&TN *for many, many years.'*
Channel 4's rival soap, Neighbourhood, *is floundering*
but promises to take the fight up to TY&TN. *Stay tuned.*

*

The Young and The Naked was one of Channel 3's biggest hits. A weekly hour-long drama which Stella Pentangeli would rather have had her liver removed with a stick than watch. However, she admired Frank String as extravagantly as his fans.

To survive 50 years in showbiz. Wow.

When they finally managed to woo Frank String into the show, the Channel 3 execs offered to have a wall of his dressing room torn down and double its size, to have the room painted, to get some 'nice furnishings' in. But Frank had graciously declined.

'I'm just an old jobbing actor,' he said with the modesty of the truly great. 'Whatever the boys and girls on the show get will be fine with me. All we actors really need is a bowl of soup and a blanket.'

Sir Rex Clap, owner of the network and a fan of any talent he owned, spent five minutes of his billionaire time inquiring how his star was settling in, then ordering Frank to accept at least a nice Italian leather couch to lay his hoar head on between scenes. 'After all, Frank, you're family now.'

*

It was early autumn and, while the rest of the town inched closer to the devil, God watched over Stella Pentangeli and inner-city Sweethurst. The trees outside Stella's beloved 6A Chatsbury Mansions apartment were purple and brown. Early leaves had cheerfully given up the ghost and fallen to the pavement to make a carpet for her feet. The sun shone every morning, brought to Sweethurst by the joy of birdsong.

Even the denizens – bohos, post-punks, the lost and the losers, the artists, artistes, actors, flim-flammer phonies and every shade of pretension and desperado in between – appeared to Stella to be fine fellows. For the first time in years, money was only a minor problem and even if it had been a major problem it wouldn't have been much of a problem.

If life gets any better I'll start skipping down Sweethurst Street like Pollyanna.

She had a habit of loftily ignoring PR handouts from anyone and everyone. The fact that she'd run the Frank String flummery in *The Pentangeli Papers* – almost word for word from Sir Rex Clap's Ministry of TV Information – was proof to the gossips that her journo juices were drying up these days.

'She's caught up in this so-called "showbiz detective" crap.'

'She's getting lazy.'

'Stella Pentangeli's never even been near the wrong end of a gun. She makes up all those criminal-catching stories and her stupid fans believe her.'

Her friends were worried about her and told her to her face.

'You're lucky you're not *dead*,' warned her business partner Terry Dear, all of 19 years old.

Investigator Ng, the object of her still-secret affections, advised: 'Stella, the only reason you are still alive is that, at critical moments, I or other police have been there with guns.'

What's Terry know? thought Stella. *He's a computer geek. He's a teenager. As for Ng, he's so beautiful. So tiny. So perfect.*

'You're always there for me, Ng,' she said. 'Why is that?'

He blushed scrutably but went on, 'It's my job. I'm a police.'

So perfect.

The only person who supported her 110 per cent was ex-police-Sgt Rodney Cross, a large red-faced brute of a man who'd attached himself to Stella and wasn't letting go. 'You're a natural born detective, Stella. And, even better, you're lucky.'

Stella had met a lot of very strange people in her showbiz journeys – first as a failed actor, then as an enfante terrible of arts criticism, then as a bitter shadow falling from showbiz grace, now as a born-again quasi-celeb detective – but Cross was one of the very strangest. He and Stella had nearly been

9

murdered several months back in pursuit of an insane killer. Cross, horribly, lost his right hand. In its place now were two opposable hooks. What to Stella would have been a vicious twist of fate was, somehow, a source of grace for Cross – as though he'd had an oversized bile duct in that very hand which, amputated, had allowed his real self to come out and play. And what a jolly self it was. Cross delighted in showing her how dextrous he was getting.

'Look, Stells. These hooks. They're great.' He picked up a saltshaker in his hooks, upended it, twisted it, turned it, played catch with it. 'See?' He took out a wooden gun he'd carved himself – a clumsy replica of his service handgun – and practised a few left-handed quick draws. 'I'm better with my left hand than I was with my right.'

Cross had started coming regularly into Sweethurst Caff, Stella's local, overpriced, noisy but necessary caffeine and breakfast hangout. Stella valued peace and privacy in her mornings but even Cross couldn't dent her well-being.

'Very good, Cross. Very good.'

'Thanks.' He turned serious and Stella knew what was coming. *He's going to nag me again about teaming up with him.*

'Your agency needs me, Stells.'

She waved an airy hand. 'There is no agency, Cross. There's just me. And I don't need a bodyguard. I'm a consulting detective. Like Sherlock Holmes.'

'Seems to me Sherlock was chased by a big dog and fell off a waterfall. You need me.'

'If I need a dog catcher near a waterfall, I'll call you, OK?' Cross smiled at her. 'It's not my BO is it?'

Big toothy smile. 'Of *course* not.'

'My breath?'

Big toothy smile strained. 'Cross. *Please.*'

'I'm using deodorant now like you said. See?' He held his

arm up to Stella's nose like an old mountain gorilla surrendering. From a reluctant distance, she sniffed.

'Perfect.'

'And mouthwash.'

'Don't breathe on me.'

Cross leant back. Gotcha. 'Stells. You need me.'

Oh Lord, staying happy is so hard.

*

Sweethurst Caff. Six weeks before. 'I will be gone for a while, Stella,' said Ng, his face giving nothing away.

'How long?' *Don't sound eager.*

'Perhaps be a week. Perhaps six months.'

'Six *months?*'

'That is rather unlikely but . . . yes.'

'Why? Where you going? What are you doing?'

But, as ever, Ng didn't answer unwanted questions and soon he had left the Caff and . . .

vanished.

*

Another six weeks before that, Ng had gone from the Caff to One Police Towers, 28 storeys high and – in its way – a monument to the success crime had always and would always enjoy in this city. As instructed, he took the Police Commissioner's private lift to the rooftop garden.

Ng had told Stella once, 'There is only one reason the Minister and the Commissioner have meetings on the roof. It is the only place guaranteed to be free of bugs and eavesdroppers.'

The mice – crims, crooked police, corrupt politicos, bent Feds – had taken over the mousetrap. The Police couldn't trust their own HQ.

Hawkeye and Connie were the only two on the roof. They sat under the ornate pagoda in comfy outdoor chairs like old soldiers during a lull in fighting. Hawkeye was Ng's immediate superior in MVC&IP (Murder, Violent Crimes and Internal Probes). Hawkeye was so named because one of his stern blue eyes was real and the other a fake. Connie was the Police Commissioner – male or female, they were always Connie. This one was a she.

'Good morning, Commissioner. Minister.'

Connie nodded. 'Ng.' She made it sound like a sneeze. 'Sit.'

Ng sat. Connie, as ever, treated Ng like part puzzle/part problem. He was by far her best murder police – one of the most famous police in the country – but he was no team player. Above a certain rank, a police was supposed to either adopt a sophisticated tolerance to high-level policio/political malfeasance or get the fuck out of the force. Ng had done neither. The media wrote:

INVESTIGATOR NG A COP'S COP

NG – HERO IN SMALL PACKAGE

Connie and a lot of police muttered:

'He's a publicity slut.'

'He's a cowboy prima donna.'

'Ng thinks he's better than us. Fuck him and his horse.'

Connie finally ventured, 'We're waiting on the Minister and another.'

Ng nodded. He didn't play office politics often, but he understood them. The Minister – Minnie, a civilian, a politician, a man – was asserting his superiority by being late.

Silence. Connie conceded another grit of information, 'We have an undercover job for you, Investigator Ng. A chance to use that Cantonese of yours.'

Ng nodded again. Silence came back.

'Ask us no questions, we'll tell you no lies,' said Hawkeye heartily, willing Ng to speak. But he and Connie both knew Ng wouldn't be asking questions. Sometimes he seemed to live in silence, saving his words and social graces for the families of clients (victims) and even for bad guys.

Connie glanced at the second elevator, the secret one that the Minister would use, and willed it to open. Nothing. She gave in and –

'You've been doing good work, Ng. Good work.'

Ng nodded, still as stone.

Hawkeye coughed.

Silence. The second elevator door opened. Minnie and a woman. Minnie – balding, bespectacled, always nervous near Connie – stepped aside to allow the woman to step onto the roof first. Ng placed her immediately. She was Deputy Commander Adrienne Lilly of the Federal Police. Mid-30s, tall, slim, buzzcut dirty blonde hair. She looked dangerous, capable, tough. She strode to the group and Minnie shuffled to keep up. To their chagrin she ignored Connie and Hawkeye. She only had eyes for Ng.

'Investigator Ng,' she said with obvious sincerity. 'I'm D.C. Lilly. I've heard so much about you. It's an honour.'

This looks like trouble, Ng thought.

D.C. Lilly went on, 'I'm forming a Federal/State task force. I want you in.'

'What's the task, Deputy Commander?'

Lilly took Ng aside. Minnie and Connie took stereo umbrage at this insulting gesture. 'Hey,' said Minnie as Connie overlapped with, 'What d'you think you're doing?'

She doesn't trust any of us bastards and she's right, Hawkeye thought, and grinned.

Lilly was unruffled. She bent down slightly to whisper

in Ng's ear, 'The task is the Fuk Chin triad and the sex slavetrade.'

Their eyes met.

'Good,' said Ng.

Lilly and Ng moved back to the group. Hawkeye waited for the fireworks.

'OK,' said Connie, cold. 'You've told Mr Ng. Now tell me.'

'Us,' said Minnie.

'Us.'

Lilly shrugged a what-can-you-do? 'Sorry, Commissioner, Minister. I'm not authorised to give out any information,' she said.

'I'm the Police Commissioner of this state, he's the Minister of Police of this state.'

'Even so.'

Hawkeye covered his mouth with a hand.

Connie's face was brick red. 'I'm not assigning Investigator Ng till I know what it's all about. And I mean *all* about what it's all about.'

Minnie followed suit. 'And I'm not having a joint task force running round my state until I'm informed of the operational parameters.'

Lilly smiled gently. She was good at games like this. 'I want two specialists in electronic surveillance seconded – Specialists Constables Savage and Webster. I'll want access to backup uniforms for muscle – no more than three dozen – at twelve hours' notice. I'll be running the show. It will be called Task Force Lincoln.'

'Last chance. What's this about, Deputy Commander?'

Lilly dropped the smile. 'Money,' she said. 'Right about now the Prime Minister and the Premier are talking. About money. The Premier wants extra federal funds for his new law and order policies. He gets his money if he cooperates.'

'The Premier would never submit to blackmail,' said Minnie loyally but without conviction; and even Connie had to smile at that.

Lilly ignored him. 'Gentlemen,' she said, indicating Hawkeye and Ng, 'would you mind stepping away for a second?'

Hawkeye rose. He and Ng moved aside. D.C. Lilly leant into Minnie and Connie and said softly, 'The Federal Minister for Justice has authorised me to say, and I quote: "If this government doesn't want me to release the findings of our inquiry into your fucked-up, pitiable, corrupt police service – with appropriate documents and videos – then give D.C. Lilly and Operation Lincoln full hands-off cooperation."' Unquote.

She sat back and waited. Connie went red. Minnie went pale.

'I'll have to speak to the Premier,' said Connie.

'Me too,' said Minnie.

The Commissioner raised her voice. 'That will be all Commander, Investigator. We'll take it from here.'

'Yes Commissioner.'

Hawkeye and Ng nodded and left the rooftop people to continue playing.

*

Six weeks.

Suddenly just a little depressed, Stella stood and said to Cross, 'I gotta go.'

'Can I have your coffee and cake?'

'Sure.'

'You gonna take me on in your agency?'

'There is no agency.'

'Please?'

'No.'

3.

RUNAWAY

Wuthering Hills is one of the older suburbs, 20 km from the city centre – part low-income housing, part factories, part stone cottages from the 1900s, all ugly.

34 Merry Street was no uglier than most. From the outside, it looked like a four-bedroom brick-veneer family house. Inside it had been gutted and remodelled to create a dozen small cubicles, each containing a cheap single bed and a wash-stand and that was about it. The three-car garage had been modified with single, double and triple decker bunks to accommodate 15 or 20 girls – all Asian, all illegal immigrants. 34 Merry Street was a big-time brothel operated by the Honourable Fuk Chin Society.

Such was the brazenness of the Chinese operators, they didn't bother to conceal the concentration-camp razor wire – three metres high all round the fence of the tiny backyard. Local lore insisted the fence was electrified but that wasn't true. Specialists V&OC (Vice and Organised Crime) knew 34 was one of a thirty-odd cheap brothels scattered round the inner and outer suburbs and that up to 200 sex slaves were involved.

They had known for two decades. They did nothing.

They knew the slaves were moved around to different houses so they wouldn't get too familiar with the local customers and the local area. They did nothing.

Many were underage. Their families in China and Thailand had sold them to the Honourable Fuk Chin Society. Others had been recruited by Fuk Chin associates to work overseas as nannies, cooks, housekeepers, whatever, then told they would work as prostitutes. Ten men a night. More. Seven days a week.

They would rape the girls to show them exactly what was required, then say, 'You owe Fuk Chin money. Work well. Work hard. In two, three years, you'll go home with enough money to buy a plot of land for your parents.'

No one. Nothing.

Two, three years would pass and the interest on the debt mounted and soon five, seven, ten years had passed and they were too old and used to be of value and when they went home, there was no home and their families turned them away.

Now and again local police would attend a complaint about 34.

They smoothed things over. They did nothing

No one. Nothing.

The high-end brothels in Vice Valley had better girls, better surroundings, spas, saunas. In Wuthering Hills, it was no frills assembly-line sex; the prices were cheap and the girls mostly clean.

*

Afterwards, no one in 34 – the pimps, the doormen, the girls, the Mother – could figure out how Bam had done it. Somehow she'd obtained pliers and snipped the razor wire enough to squeeze through, leaving hunks of dress and flesh behind. Bam was 23. Everyone called her Bum because she wasn't pretty and specialised in anal sex.

Bam had recently been traded from the Happy Hills brothel and had never been beyond its backyard. A stranger in a strange land. So she just ran – first down a tiny alley, then onto a well-lit main road where trucks and cars dodged her. BEEP. HONK. SCREECH. Across the road at full pelt. BEEP. HONK. 'DUMB BITCH.' She ran and ran till her lungs caught fire and her legs shook even as she ran.

HONK. 'BAM. COME.' She turned her head and there they were – two Fuk Chin bouncers from 34 in a black car. She veered into a side street and SCREECH, she heard the car follow. What a fool I am, she thought. I should have stayed on the big road where there are people.

'BAM. STOP. COME.' But she kept running. Maybe they would shoot her. That would be good.

WE-ARE. WE-ARE. WE-ARE. Bam saw – thank you Lord Buddha – flashing lights and a siren as a police patrol car headed towards them from the opposite end of the street. The black car stopped. The police car came to a halt and the siren wound down.

WEEEEEaarrrrrr.

Bam rushed up to the police as they exited the car. 'Help. Must help. Pr'oner. Unnerstan'? Locked up. Unnerstan'?'

'Calm down, Miss. We're here to help.'

'Yes. Help.'

The uniforms took in her scratched body and ragged clothes, got out their guns and headed for the black car. 'You two. Out. Keep your hands in plain sight. Out.'

Dutifully, the Fuk Chins got out.

'Hands.'

They showed meek hands to the police. 'See, Off'cers? Emp'y.'

'Hands behind neck, turn away, kneel down.'

They knelt with ease and grace. They'd done this before. First uniform kept his gun trained on both kneeling men as second uniform, careful to stay out of the firing line, patted the men down. Each had a gun. Same model. Glocks.

'Permit. Gun. Permit. Unn'stand?' one of the Fuks said.

First uniform ignored him, cuffed their hands behind their backs. The Fuks seemed content to kneel there forever. Second uniform took their wallets and headed back to the police car.

Bam was sitting next to the car, her legs vibrating uncontrollably. Some of the girls had told her the police in this country were different, that she could trust them, that it was not like back home. Bam never believed them. No matter the country, a policeman follows only the orders of the people who have money. She'd been a fool to run. Mother and the men would beat her for that. The new razor-wire scars would lower her price even more. Mother and the men would beat her for that, too. Fool, she was. Fool.

'Don't you worry, Miss,' said first uniform. He opened the boot of the police car. Most suburban uniforms carried a spare blanket or two in case they got some snooze time. He wrapped one gently around her and Bam realised this man – this policeman – *a policeman?* – was the first person who had been gentle with her since . . .

. . . since never.

She listened as second uniform spoke into the police radio. Most of it she couldn't understand but she saw him get angrier, then slam down the radio mic, breaking it. He looked at Bam. She saw shame in his eyes and then she knew.

'Uncuff em and give em back their guns,' said second uniform.

'What?'

'They're Ma's people.'

'What about the woman?'

'Give her back.' Bile in each syllable.

First uniform took the cash from the Fuks' wallets, and pocketed it, tossed the wallets on the ground. The men picked them up and accepted their guns back with modest and grateful 'Tank you, sirs.'

First uniform was praying the woman would read the signs and make a run for it. Run. Hide. He and his partner will find her later and get her the hell away from this. But Bam had given up. She patiently folded up the blanket, gave it to the uniforms, walked over to the men.

'In car, Bam.'

She didn't look at them, nor at the policeman – not even the gentle one, who'd lied with his eyes that he would help her. She got in the back seat like a lamb and the police watched as the men drove off with the Honourable Society's property.

Not for the first time, first uniform thought of kicking the whole deal and quitting the force. Why not? Why bother? Second uniform gave him his half of the money from the Fuks' wallets. They pocketed six thousand dollars each.

Ah well.

*

A pet bull terrier found Bam's body in a shallow grave in a seldom-used part of Wuthering Hills Park the next day. The dog's owner had to pry Bam's nose loose from the hungry and furious mutt.

The City Press tried to make a big deal out of it. A crusade.

ASIAN GIRL FOUND MURDERED.
WAS SHE PART OF SEX SLAVE RING?
The body of an unknown . . .

YOU'VE GOT TO BE KIDDING. NO SEX SLAVES?

SEX SLAVES CLAIMS ARE 'RACIST SMEARS'.
The Chinese Cultural Association spokesman, Ms Yu, said she regarded The City Press's *accusations as 'blatant racism and . . .'*

The Premier was adamant in his denial. 'There never have been and never will be and are not now any quote unquote "sex slave rings" in this state. It's . . .'

No one cared. No one knew her name. *The City Press* gave up. The crusade fizzled out. Hawkeye gave the Asian-unknown-female-client event to Investigator Bell and Sgt Bukowski. They came up with nothing. Since no one had claimed her body, the state buried her cheap.

4.

THE YOUNG AND THE

NAKED WRITER

Stella sat in her apartment, trying not to be moody. The over-the-top joy she'd been feeling lately had moved out of her heart and was hiding somewhere. Try as she might, she couldn't quite track it down.

Come back. I need you.

But there was no reply. Stella figured she may as well write some showbiz for *The Pentangeli Papers*. She popped open her laptop with reluctant fingers. Her phone rang. She answered gratefully. 'Pentangeli.'

'Stella, it's Norman Huffman.'

'Who?'

'Huffman. Norman Huffman.'

Huffman? Ahhhh.

*

Norman Huffman was Sir Rex Clap's personal lackey. If he'd ever had an original thought, a life of his own or, indeed, a backbone, he'd long given them all to Sir Rex on permanent loan.

Stella had worked for Sir Rex way way way back and even then Norman had been wiping his master's bottom and rejoicing in it. Stella's TV arts show, *S for Showbiz!* had

made many millions for Sir Rex and he had rewarded her
by cancelling her gig in *S4S!* and replacing her with a tits-
and-teeth blonde called Cookie Creeme.

And the reason she got canned?

Hair.

Her red hair had turned white. Overnight. After learning
that her mother and father – estranged and strangers to her
now – had been killed in a hit-and-run in the country. At
the cremation service, Norman weaselled her aside.

'I've arranged a hairdressing appointment for next week.'

Stella looked at Norman. One of them was hallucinating.
'What?'

'A hairdresser. Next week.'

'Why?'

Norman looked at her with sympathy. Poor thing. Just
buried her parents. Her memory was strained. 'Stella,' he
cooed, 'you said you want to get straight back to work.'

'I do.'

'You'll have to get your hair dyed.'

'Why?'

'Why?'

'Yes. Why?'

'It's grey. No, white.'

'So?'

'Sir Rex wants you to dye your hair.'

'No.'

'Stella . . .'

'I'm not dyeing my fucking hair.'

Silence. Hmm.

That night, Norman dropped round to Chatsbury Mansions.
Stella knew he was bringing orders from the master. 'Sir Rex
wants to make some changes to *S4S!* Sir Rex wants to take
Channel 3 up-market.'

'Clap thinks up-market is naked chicks doing the can-can with roses up their ...'

'Ah, so you needn't come back to the studio. We'll pay out your contract, of course – minus expenses. Sir Rex sends his deepest sympathies in your hour of sorrow.'

'I want to speak to the prick.'

'He'll be in England for the next few weeks.'

'Bullshit. I can smell him from here. Tell him to stick his deepest sympathies.'

Thus ended Stella Pentangeli's status as a major player in showbiz, TVbiz and, well, life, really.

*

'Norman. Of course I remember you.'

'Can you come see us?' said Norman.

'Why should I?'

'Because,' said Norman, 'we have a detective job for the lady showbiz detective.'

'Why me?'

'Why not? Sir Rex has heard you're good.'

Stella sighed, pretending irritation but preening her ego feathers. 'OK. When?'

'Today.'

'When?'

'Now.' Norman was insistent. 'At the Channel. Sir Rex told me to tell you he'll make it worth your while.'

Pause. 'I'll have to rearrange my diary.' *Yeah, right.*

'It's urgent, Stella.'

'Gimme an hour.'

'Don't drive in. Park in the street. South gate. Keep low. I'll come get you.'

'What do you mean – keep low?'

'Undercover. You mustn't be seen.'

'OK Norman.' *TV people. Drama queens all.*

She hung up before he did something silly like tell her to wear a disguise or take an oath.

*

'I'd like you to wear this disguise and I need you to promise everything you hear will remain secret.'

Norman held out a red polka-dot scarf and a massive pair of sunglasses as he blocked the VW door, preventing her from getting out. He was as slim and slimy as ever but his hair was thinner and suspiciously black; his face was neutral but his voice didn't like her.

'Sir Rex insists.'

'Why is it, d'you think, Norman?'

'Why what?'

'Why do TV people live on the craziest rung of showbiz?'

'You must promise,' Norman insisted.

'I promise. Scout's honour.' *TV people.*

*

'Jesus, Pentangeli. You look like a movie star in that get-up,' said Sir Rex, his voice all gravel, power and expensive brandy.

'Thank you, Sir Rex.' Stella took off the scarf and sunglasses and looked at her lowlife ex-employer. Sir Rex was 60, barrel-chested, with cold eyes sunk in a pale wide face. His lips were red chunks of prime steak and he had an air of being the owner of wherever he was.

He was a bully at school. It worked. He never changed.

'Wanna drink? I'm having brandy. Norman. Double. Balloon. Warm.'

'It's a bit early for . . . OK. Beefeater. Rocks.'

'Make it a double, Norman.'

Norman glided to the oversized bar – New Orleans, 1920s – as Stella glanced around Clap's office. The essentials hadn't changed. The mahogany and leather and steel were all as polished and abundant; just the knickknacks – smaller phones, bigger TV screens, smaller computers – were updated. As ever, Sir Rex kept the bathroom door ajar, the better for visitors to see the marble and gold fittings.

'Siddown.'

Stella sank into a seat. Sir Rex got up, rounded the desk and rested his ample rump on it.

'So. I hear you're a private detective now. I hear you're a good one.'

It was true. Her reputation was fine. Apart from two better-documented and lethal cases, she'd worked on half a dozen showbiz trifles as investigator and/or consultant. Cross was right. She *was* a natural born detective.

'I do OK, Sir Rex.'

She took a bucket of Beefeater from Norman's tray and tried not to enjoy it too obviously. Clap downed his bucket in a swallow.

'Norman. 'Nother.'

Norman was already offering it. Clap took a swallow then frowned at Stella as though the brandy wasn't good enough and it was her fault.

'Channel 4 is stealing our *Young and Naked* scripts,' he said.

'It's a major, major problem,' added Norman, shaking his head in disgust. 'It's getting to the point where *Neighbourhood* is getting our stolen stories on air *before us*. It makes it look like *we're* stealing *their* ideas.'

Neighbourhood was one of Channel 4's few major hits. It was 30 commercial minutes (i.e. 22 minutes), five nights a week, 40 weeks a year. It was even crummier than *TY&TN* but the critics had decided it was getting 'better' and –

worse – it was fast catching up to *The Young and The Naked* in the ratings.

'It's thievery,' said Norman. 'It's a disgrace.'

'Fuck off, Norman,' said Sir Rex. 'I'll call you if I need you.'

'Certainly, sir.' Norman exited the office with admirable dignity. *He's the butler*, thought Stella, idly. *The butler always did it.*

Sir Rex finished his drink, fisted his glass down on the desk, pointed his finger at Stella. 'OK, Pentangeli, here's what I want you to do. I . . .'

'Whoa. Just a minute.'

Sir Rex stopped, surprised. In his whole life he'd never been whoa-ed. Stella took a sip of her Beefeater, savouring the moment. Then: 'I haven't taken the job yet (sip). I'm not some airhead anchorette now (sip). I don't know if I want to work for you.'

'You get fifty grand upfront.'

Wow!

Stella knew 50 thousand dollars was almost meaningless to Sir Rex. He'd once dropped three million dollars in an hour at City Casino but still . . .

Wow!

'When you find the leak, you get another fifty grand.'

Note to self: never steal from a billionaire. They'll pay someone to hunt you down, then they'll kill you and eat you.

'A hundred sounds fair,' she said, keeping her voice steady-ish. 'What do you want me to do?'

Clap had put a lot of thought into this. 'Things have changed since your day as far as soaps go. Of course, if I had my way I'd stop making home-grown shit and buy em from the USA and Britain like God intended. But . . .' He shrugged.

He owned a big chunk of the State Government but could only rent the Feds on a case-by-case basis. The Feds knew that the voters, who loved NYPD brutality and London romances and sitcoms, also wanted a bit of their own culture reflected back at them. If he wanted to keep his licence, Sir Rex knew he had to churn out *some* local product – however grudgingly.

'We got thirty-three countries taking *Naked* now. It's top five in *all* those countries. *All of em.*'

Stella knew all this. She also knew that the pride in Clap's eyes wasn't because he'd made a quality, relevant show; it was because 33 countries were sending him mountains of extra money for nothing.

'It's all Mo Sherlock's doing,' he said.

Stella had already guessed that. But, for a hundred thou, she'd listen to Clap recite ''Twas On The Good Ship Venus'.

'She stole a couple of my *Balls* stars.'

Balls was Channel 3's other big-time drama – one hour of tits and bums and sweat and pecs a week – set in the world of professional sport.

'So? *You* steal talent all the time.'

'That's business. This is *betrayal*. Mo's got someone *right here in my Channel 3 family betraying me.*'

'Why don't you sue? Theft of intellectual property. Whatever.'

Clap looked suddenly shifty. 'The lawyers say it's hard to prove.'

There's more. Stella's mouth was dry. *There's more.*

'Plus?'

'Plus? Plus what?'

'Plus why else?'

Sir Rex's face clouded over. 'That cow Sherlock's not getting Rex Clap to go to court.'

'Why not?'

'Cos even if I win the case, I lose.'

'Why?'

Clap looked at Stella as though she were a mental retard who'd wandered into the conversation. 'Why? Cos she's a fucking *woman*.'

Ah yes. Of course.

*

In the beginning was the word and the words of *The Young and The Naked* began with Elias Zwik. Zwikky was – by all accounts, including his own – a genius. It was he who, ten years previously, came up with the notion of a sitcom called *The Iscariots*. Set in AD 30, it told amusing domestic tales of Judas Iscariot, a hard-working family man with a nagging but loving wife, a sulky but loving teenage daughter, a wise-cracking but loving younger son, a discontented but loving housekeeper slave and a manic-depressive boarder called Jesus Christ. Naturally, all the stations and production houses passed on even filming a pilot of such a nauseatingly blasphemous and offensive idea. Many didn't even want to touch the paper it was *written on*. In a couple of instances, Zwikky was physically assaulted.

Clap heard about the young man and summoned him to his office, much as Stella had been summoned a decade later. Zwikky pitched the idea. He knew the old fart would hate it.

Sir Rex loved it. He promptly fired Channel 3's Head of Comedy – who had been one of the most grievously offended by The Iscariots – and installed Zwikky in his place. Clap gambled that, even if The Iscariots turned out to be a turkey, it would get lots of ink and signify that Channel 3 was after the 'young, edgy and up yours' market. The show worked as cult, got the rich hip demographics and ran three seasons.

Zwikky came to the channel just as the golden age of Channel 3 was about to turn platinum. Stella, in her mid-20s, flame-haired and lush, was the most popular female anchor on the box. In rapid succession, Zwikky created the new soap *Balls* and the hugely popular quiz show *Answer The Question!* The Heads of Drama and Light Entertainment complained about Zwikky's sticking his thumb in their pies. Sir Rex demoted them both and had them report to Zwikky, making one of his little jokes: 'From now on, Zwikky's SLOEWM – Supreme Lord of Everything We Make. If SLOEWM don't OK it, it's not OK.'

Then Zwikky handed his boss *the* masterpiece – the mother lode, the show of shows – *The Young and The Naked.*

TY&TN had a simple message – youth, money, beauty and power can change you into a god and, in this vale of tears, happiness is good but money is better. The public bought it right away. As Stella – queen of the TV pundits – put it, Why *not* buy the show's central theme? It's as good a philosophy as anyone else has come up with lately.

The Iscariots, Balls, Answer The Question!, TY&TN and a string of game shows, soaps, mini-series. Zwikky laid all these treasures at Sir Rex's feet. In turn, Sir Rex gave Zwikky money and power and – to the dismay of Clap's Machiavellian daughter, Goneril, and his half-bright son, Randy – even love.

∗

Clap's office door opened. Stella turned to see Elias Zwik enter.

'Zwikky,' said Clap warmly.

'Sir Rex.' Equally warmly.

'You remember Stella Pentangeli?'

Zwik moved to her. 'Remember her? Stella Five Angels?

I was desperately in love with her and she never gave me the time of day.'

Which was sort of true. In the first flush of success, the too-young Zwik rightfully assumed that his perks included any woman he could get his hands on, or more often, any woman who could get her hands on him.

Stella took him in. About 30. The fingers of his right hand were stained brown. He was a smoker.

All day meetings would be hell for him.

Thick brown curly hair antennaed in all directions. One ring – a big silver skull's head. His clothes a step away from Salvation Army donations yet, his laptop was top-of-the-line.

Still a boho-hippie-punk and still proud of it.

'Seems to me,' said Stella, 'you had women falling before you like corn stalks before a thrasher.'

'Hey. What a great image. Sir Rex, let's hire her.'

'She's already hired, remember?'

'Oh yeah. That's right.' He looked at her. 'You're our spy.'

*

Coffee machine. Cakes. Long table. Whiteboard. A sign on the door: 'DO NOT DISTURB. EVER.'

'Listen up.'

Everyone in the writers' room froze at the sound of Sir Rex's voice. Stella and Zwikky stood either side of him.

'We have Stella Pentangeli with us today. She's going to do a piece about *Naked* for her online thing. It's feel-good powder-puff bumph so don't go airing any of *my* dirty laundry.'

They laughed dutifully. The old bull trundled away. The writing staff – two men and a young woman – looked at her like she was an exotic bug who belonged to the king. Zwikky pointed at the men.

'This is Walter. This is William. This is Stella Pentangeli from *The Pentangeli Papers*.'

'Walter. William.'

'Hello,' they said in perfect unison.

He pointed at the girl – 19, petite, foxy, just-punk-enough-for-a-business-office. 'This is Ricci-Trish.'

'Yo,' said Ricci-Trish in a straight-outta-da-hood accent.

'Ricci-Trish,' said Stella.

'The W's and I are the writers. Ricci-Trish is note-taker, researcher, typist and voice of youth.'

'Where are the rest of you?'

Hesitation wafted into the room. Stella jumped in with the words that she, Zwik and Sir Rex had agreed on: 'Listen. Sir Rex is buying advertising on *TPP*. Big bucks. I need the money. Nothing bad leaves this room. OK? Like Sir Rex said, it's powder-puff.'

They looked at her. Then relaxed.

'There is no "rest of you",' said Walter.

'None,' said William.

'Zwikky's terminated everyone else,' said Walter.

'Everyone,' echoed William.

'Just us.'

'Just us.'

Walter and William. They've mind-melded, thought Stella. *They're soap writers who signed up for life and have slowly and become one person.*

'But why?' asked Stella, all wide-eyed innocence.

Zwikky pretended reluctance. 'Our storylines are being stolen.'

Stella pretended surprise. 'Stolen? You four are writing *all the episodes?*' It was the equivalent of writing a full-length movie every two weeks.

'We're on a wartime footing,' said Ricci-Trish proudly. 'Till we catch the thieves.'

'But that's a secret,' said William.

'Top secret,' said Walter.

'Of course.' Stella sat at the long table. 'Just go on like I'm not here. I'm a fly on the wall.'

'OK,' said Zwikky, turning into Mr Efficiency. 'Sit. Turn the Artistic Amplifiers to eleven and let's rock and roll.'

They sat. The room was suddenly all business. Episode 300 of *TY&TN* would be mapped out today and – landmark that it was – 300 had to be a doozy. Zwikky, Ricci-Trish and the W's had mapped out a storyline.

The A story: gruff but gentle old Harold Bellbird is kidnapped by a sexy terrorist. Story B: a barely post-pubescent teen girl (Brooke Rivers) and her racing horse (Thunder) finally bond.

'Ricci-Trish. Before I forget. Make sure Thunder's a watchamacallit? – a lady horse.'

'A mare?' said Ricci-Trish.

'Yeah. We don't want sweet little innocent Brooke Rivers dismounting and finding herself eye-to-eye with a big fucking horse schlong.'

Oh God. It's going to be a long day.

5.

DAY OF THE RUSSIANS

Cross lingered at the Caff. He liked it there. Twice-divorced, nearing 60, unattached, with a comfortable police pension, he'd taken a late-life what-now? crisis and transformed it into a move into the inner-city where he rented a furnished studio apartment in West Sweethurst. His new-found good nature – after a lifetime of bad – held firm and he found, to his delight, he was welcomed into the arty bohodom that was Sweethurst society. Cross – the guy with the rotating hooks instead of a right hand; Cross, who talked like a gangster and dressed like a door-to-door salesman (with pork-pie hat), was very quickly a bona fide Sweethurst character. Uncle Rodney.

Cross was also more than happy to use his old police juice to get the odd Sweethurstian out of minor problems with the law and he could always be relied on to listen to young people's problems and give them blunt advice of the pithy 'Stop doing it.' or 'Go fucking apologise.' or 'Be a man.' variety.

Some girls, in particular, were attracted to his over-the-top masculinity. In a world of middle-class effeteness and testosterone deficiency, they dug his style, his hooks-instead-of-hand, and he loved nothing more than to scare the wide-eyed does with the tale of how his hand was 'hacked off by this fucking maniac and used in a Shakespeare ritual murder as a fucking candle-holder.' Women with a *penchant* for father figures found in Cross a triple-strength Big Daddy. Some came back to his studio and some stayed a night or three.

The Day of the Russians – today – turned him from a character into a bona fide Sweethurst star.

*

Cross noted but disregarded the fair-haired man in cheap clothes who entered the Sweethurst Caff, went to the counter and asked in an East European accent to see the owner, Mona. Cross saw Mona and the man enter the back room office. Five minutes later the man exited the office grinning and Mona exited, red-eyed and upset. Cross made an instant decision. He rushed to Mona. 'What happened? Quick.'

Mona tried. 'That man . . .' She couldn't finish.

'Did he extort money?'

'He's a Russian. He said he's Mafia. He's coming back tomorrow. He said he'd firebomb the place if . . .'

But Cross was already out the door. He spotted the man on the street. He'd evidently just paid a similar visit to Simon de Sweethurst's Hair Studio.

*

Cross remembered talk of this wannabe Russian Mafia crew from his final police days.

'These Russian bozos have hit town and . . .'

'They'd rather shoot a man than have a good meal.'

'Doc or Ma will cream em.'

*

35

'Hey,' said Cross in his best friendly manner.

The man turned calmly, not a care in the world. Cross joined him.

'What's your name, Boris?'

The man smiled sweetly. 'Boris is not name. Boris is cartoon name for Russian. I am Georgian. I soon am citizen. Call me Sir.'

'No,' said Cross, 'I think I'll call you Boris, Boris.'

Boris shook his head sadly, astonished at the perversity – the self-destructive silliness – of some people. He jerked his head at a beat-up car across the street. Two swarthy men looked their way. 'Those men. They my friends. You go way now or they come here look what happen.'

'Hey,' Cross yelled across the street. 'Come join us, fellas.'

The two men in the car looked startled, then obligingly got out of the car and headed for Cross and Boris. Their clothes were tight, the height of 1970's hip.

'Great to see you. And you!' roared Cross in a best-buddy bar-room boom and suddenly, surprisingly, gave each of the newcomers a hug. The hugs were over and done with before they could take offence.

They're not armed, thought Cross. Which makes sense. A weapons charge is the last thing they'd want while trying to set up shop. Still, the police grapevine was correct. These guys were dumb as mud and half as heavy. Boris 1 rattled off a string of stuff to Borises 2 and 3, which Cross assumed was a quick summary of how this big stupid one-handed hero was the perfect fall guy to impress the shopkeepers with how deadly serious the Borises were. Cross could smell it. The Borises had made their decision. We'll beat the shit out of him here and now – maybe even kill him.

Boris 2 was sneaking ever-so-subtly to Cross's rear right.

'So talk,' said Boris 1. 'We all ears.'

'Not anymore.'

Cross twisted his hooks just a tad and lashed out at 2, taking off his ear with surgical precision. Even as the ear fell to the ground and they watched in disbelief, Cross delivered his trademark Cross Kick Balls Special which involved stepping back slightly, then, his leg fully extended for maximum torque, smashing his size-13 boot at full power up and into the groin of 3, who went down. 2 was on his knees cupping his precious severed ear in both hands. Boris 1 stood his ground but only till Cross twisted his hooks again and this time, the Russian had a razor sharp tip at his throat. An upward thrust from Cross would likely take off his jaw.

Cross spoke slowly into 1's face. 'These are my streets. These are my people. You wanna shake some people down, go somewhere else – a long way somewhere else. Understand?'

'Sure. We do that.'

'You promise?'

'Sure. Promise. On grave. On mother's eyes.'

'OK.'

'OK.'

'Bye now.'

Cross grinned at the three Borises and waved as they hurried to their old car and drove off. Cross felt his face with his left hand. No sweat. His hand trembled but that was expected in these types of adrenalin situations. A spattering of applause made him turn. Mona and a bunch of Caff patrons, Simon and a bunch of salon patrons and a large gathering of onlookers cheered and whistled from across the street. Cross bowed low, from the waist. Thank you, thank you. PoliceBiz *can* be fun. With a heroic *adios* and a salute ('My work here is done. Come, Tonto'), he strolled off towards his studio flat, knowing that at least one of those applauding was already on the phone to rat him out to the cops.

He knew, too, that some police would come round to see him and – in the tradition of the city – find him innocent of everything and maybe buy him a beer or three at The Cop Bar.

He also knew another thing. Those Russian clowns were dead meat. Babes in the woods. Doc Mortaferi or Mr Ma would wrap them up in bloody shrouds and throw them down this pit they had just near Hades from where no one ever returned.

He sort of kind of felt sorry for the bastards.

*

And so he should have.

*

Stella's partner, Terry Dear, caught the Cross v Russian whisper and – as so often these days – cluck-clucked at Stella's woeful inattention to her own zine and wrote a piece.

SHOWBIZ! SHOWBIZ! SHOWBIZ! ONLINE!
THE PENTANGELI PAPERS ***EXCLUSIVE***!
CRIMEBIZ: WHO WAS THAT HOOKED MAN?
by Terry Dear
It looks like Sweethurst, home to the glitterati, literati and
mediocriti has found a new superhero.
Ex-cop Sgt Rodney Cross, who has recently made Luvvie Heaven
his home, single-handedly faced down a brazen extortion gang
right here in beautiful downtown Sweethurst and, as they
say, kicked arse like Batman's bigger brother.
If you come across a giant of a man with two hooks for a right
hand, you might want to shake the left one.
Rodney Cross, Sweethurst welcomes you.

6.

DOC AND MA

Some days are diamond.

Doc Mortaferi gazes out the one-way-view plate window of his Bayside Bay mansion. Floor to ceiling and 200 degrees of sight. Dusk. Mortaferi's favourite time of day. Clouds catch the last rays and turn them pink-edged; sea gulls make frenzied preparations for a sleepy night; the sea turns purple; if there are strong winds, a thousand streaks of white slash the purple near the shore. The sun is gone now and the sea's trying to hide. Purple turns black. The doorbell rings.

'Right on time,' says Mortaferi.

What looks and sounds like an English butler glides to the entrance, checks the security-cam and opens the oak door.

'Alfred,' says Mr Ma.

'Sir,' says Alfred, then – a nod from Mortaferi – disappears into the back of the mansion. Mortaferi strides across the huge living room with its too-polished wood floors.

'Ma.'

'Doc.'

Doc believes in the personal touch. He fetches Ma's drink himself. Soda water. Doc decides to follow suit. Tonight's too important for fuzzy thinking. They sit in Doc's too-large calf-hide chairs and size each other up. As usual, each likes what he sees.

Ma is above average height, stocky and built strong. He wears a pin-stripe banker's suit. Saville Row. An emerald ring on his pinkie.

Mortaferi is tanned and buff. Expensive but casual slacks and shirt. A massive chunk of gold round his neck. Hollywood hair. For all that, they are both serious men.

Mortaferi's Australian crew runs and licenses all criminal activity in the city. Ma is the only man Doc fears. For a token percentage, Mortaferi lets Fuk Chin handle the Asian end of gambling, standover, drugs, prostitution and the rest. The round-eye trade is plenty for Mortaferi and, even if it weren't, the only alternative would be a war between the two crews and it would be disastrous for both.

'Happy days.'

'Mud in your eye, Doc.'

They sip.

'So, Ma, how can I be of help?'

'I'll be needing your boatshed.'

*

Ma is saying that he'll be needing Mortaferi's body disposal service – his boatshed – fast and foolproof.

The boatshed body disposal service – along with Doc's two-way-mirror-and-video brothels – are the foundation of his pre-eminence in the city's criminal elite.

In theory, Mortaferi is a keen fisherman, yachting enthusiast and man of the sea. In fact, Doc prefers his fish served in high class restaurants, suffers *mal de mer* in any but the calmest seas and perfects his suntan by his pool.

In theory, the boatshed is all there for Doc's great love –

the 25-metre cruiser, 'Doc's Pride'. The boatshed is where his lady is pampered and scrubbed and de-barnacled.

In fact, the boatshed's true value is as the place where bodies are dismembered and packed neatly into large fine-mesh cages; and the trace evidence is flushed straight down the sloping tiles into the open sea. The cages are taken out to sea and dumped overboard.

*

'Of course, my old friend,' says Doc to Ma. 'Anything.'

'I will, of course, pay for your services,' says Mr Ma.

Doc waves a negligent hand. That's understood. Ma is an honourable man. So are they both; both honourable men.

'How many . . . customers?'

'One, six, a dozen maybe.'

It's true. 'So you *are* going after the Russians.'

Ma shrugs noncommittally. Doc has heard about this small but irritating Russian gang which has recently taken up residence in the city. They lack a politico/policio power base. They have a tendency to unnecessary violence. They wander into other crews' territories and bring their muscle and guns. They attract attention. They're a nuisance and they're dispensable.

'You are, aren't you?'

Ma sighs. 'Blood and bullying sadden me, Doc. I know they sadden you. They interfere with our commerce; but these Russians *delight* in blood. I even summoned them for a talk. I asked them to stop being so disruptive. They refused. They laughed in my face. I think it's time I made them go away.' (i.e. 'I think it's time I had them slaughtered.')

'You need a hand?'

'This is Fuk Chin business.' (i.e. 'This is my business. These clownish barbarians are mine. They insulted me. They die.')

Some days *are* diamond. For the past few weeks, Doc had been urged by friends of friends of people close to the government and the legal system to take out the Russians himself. Doc had started planning. Now Ma would take care of the wet end and Doc would make a nice profit from them after all.

'Another drink, Ma?'

'Please.'

'Got time for a few games of backgammon?'

'Excellent. Excellent,' says Mr Ma. 'I thought you'd never ask.'

They both love the game and are good at it. Doc is one of the few round-eyes Ma has met who plays as well as he.

7.

PLOTS AND STRATAGEMS

Stella had been right. It was a long, long day plotting how Harold Bellbird would fall into the hands of Irish terrorists led by a mysterious Major Phineas we don't see till EP 301 who turns out to be nada nada and they're not *really* terrorists, they're nada nada and what they *really* want is nada nada. Meanwhile, pretty young Brooke Rivers is thrown from her genderless horse, Thunder, while riding the windswept plains of the Bellbird Estate and nada nada nada.

It turned out that Zwikky was not at all discomfited by any Channel 3 smoking bans. He just ignored them and — such was his clout — nobody said a word. Now and then Ricci-Trish would cough meaningfully and open the windows. When it got breezy, Zwikky would close them even as he continued to talk through the plot points and the characters' motives. An hour or so later, the dance of smoke and windows would begin again.

If anyone even tried to stop him smoking, he'd get up and walk; and there'd be a dozen production houses who'd snap him right up and lick out the ashtrays.

For the first time, really, since she met Ng, Stella found

herself attracted to someone. Elias Zwik smelt like an ashtray and looked like a bum. He wasted his talent on TV shit and – sure enough – come noon, he pulled out an oversized silver flask of something strong, and sipped on it for the rest of the day. He was arrogant and self-opiniated. He didn't give a damn.

And so cute.

Finally, in a haze of smoke, terrorism, horses and cliff-hangers, the script conference ended.

*

Stella, Clap, Zwikky and Norman met in the big office for what Norman grandly dubbed 'a debriefing'.

Sir Rex jumped into the deep end. 'So, Pentangeli, waddaya got?'

Stella glanced discreetly at Zwikky. 'Perhaps I should speak to you alone.'

Clap disposed of Stella's subtlety with his usual grace. 'Zwikky,' he said, 'I sent Pentangeli to spy on you.'

Zwikky gave Stella a more-in-amusement-than-anger look. Very soulful. 'I should have guessed.'

'No offence, Zwikky.'

'None taken.'

'Siddown. Norman. Get drinks.'

'Yes, sir. The usual, everyone?'

Everyone nodded vaguely in Norman's direction and he fussed about behind the bar as Sir Rex repeated: 'So, Pentangeli, waddaya got?'

'Walter and William don't register on my radar,' said Stella. 'They're lifers. They're adding machines. They're workhorses who haul people like Zwikky up the soap mountain.'

'"Soap mountain",' said Zwik. 'Hey, Miss Five Angels, that's good.'

'I got a million of em.'

'I want to hear them all.'

'You will.'

Clap clicked teeth in irritation. 'Get on with it.'

Stella got on with it. 'I figure the W's wouldn't know a dramatic idea if it bit them on their arses. I figure they're lucky to have their jobs. I figure they'd never risk them. I also figure they'd be too scared of Sir Rex to betray him.'

Zwikky nodded. Clap grunted. Norman laid out the drinks. They drank.

'What about me. Am I the traitor?' said Zwik.

Clap laughed. 'If you're the traitor, Zwikky, I'm fucked. I may as well fold up the drama department, shoot you and slit my throat.'

Clap beamed at Zwikky who smiled back.

Clap loves him, thought Stella. *He's the son he never had.*

'I don't think you're the traitor, Zwikky,' she said.

'Why not?' He lit a cigarette which Clap and Norman ignored.

'You don't need to steal ideas from yourself. You got plenty.'

'You can say that again,' said Clap proudly.

'You could make more money giving Mo Sherlock a few brand new ones. Plus, I figure your salary and perks at 3 are good. Plus, I figure here you have absolute power. Why risk it?'

Zwikky nodded thoughtfully. 'Sounds right.'

'So, is it that little punk chick?' asked Clap. 'With the pierced tits?'

'Ricci-Trish,' said Zwikky.

Stella paused. If she'd been as honest with herself as she'd been with the others she'd have said, *Ricci-fucking-Trish treated me like I'm an old woman. Ricci-fucking-Trish is young and pretty and wears a belly-revealing top to highlight gold studs piercing a perfect belly button. She has nipple rings piercing the perfect nipples of her perfect breasts and doesn't need a bra.*

If there were a God, the spy would be Ricci-Trish.

Instead, she said: 'It makes sense. I'd guess she doesn't get paid much.'

'She gets paid very well,' Sir Rex protested. 'She's family.'

'Yeah, right,' said Zwikky, waving his empty glass at Norman. 'Let's face it, no one is *ever* paid enough. *Ever.* It could be an actor, director, writer, stagehand, girlfriend, boyfriend. Maybe Mo Sherlock's bugged the place. Who knows?'

Stella's mouth went dry, as it usually did when a plot — a brilliant stratagem — was heading her way.

Zwikky continued. 'These are *ideas* we're dealing with here. How do you find an *ideas* thief?'

Stella's idea landed. 'We turn ideas into booby-traps,' she said. 'We turn ideas into a mousetrap.'

They looked at her.

Clap: 'You want to speak English, Pentangeli?'

'*Certainment.* Zwikky, what's the EP 300 cliffhanger?' She shivered with delight at her canniness.

Zwikky frowned. 'Erm ... we got two cliffhangers. One: Harold Bellbird is kidnapped by terrorists. Two: Brooke is thrown off her horse. Is she dead or not?'

'OK,' said Stella, fired up, 'we create, right now, right here in this room, four sets of fake cliffhangers for EP 300. One set each for Walter, William and Ricci-Trish. A fourth set for the actors and crew. I find out what Mo's heard and we've got our guy. At least we know if it's cast, crew or writers.'

Zwikky jumped on the idea, lighting a new cigarette off the old.

'Excellent.'

He started pacing as he thought and he was suddenly alive times ten.

He's on fire.

'Take this down, someone.'

I like fire.

Norman picked up pen and paper as, incredibly, Elias Zwik, off the top of his head, rattled out four brand new sets of authentic-sounding fake cliffhangers to bait a mousetrap and catch a rat.

Norman himself typed up the four new sets and photocopied one each of Sets #1, #2 and #3 and a dozen of Set #4 to be carefully distributed to the actors.

Cast:

From Writers

Forward planning. Keep this quiet from EVERYONE. Repeat EVERYONE. EP 300 will be a big one.

Harold Bellbird, who has recovered his memory, marries the very young nurse, Casey, who helped him in the nuthouse.

Brooke finds her beloved new horse, Thunder, has been decapitated and the head left in her school locker.

Be advised that this is ultra-ultra secret. PLEASE. Channel 4 has messed us around enough.

Cheers,

Elias.

Ricci-Trish got this –

Forward planning. EP 300. Keep this quiet, even from the W's.

Harold has a heart attack.

Brooke runs off with her English Teacher.

W1 got –

Forward planning. EP 300. Keep this quiet, even from Ricci-Trish and W.
   Harold discovers his accountants have left him penniless.
   Brooke decides to become a nun.

W2 got –

Forward planning. EP 300. Keep this quiet, even from Ricci-Trish and W.
   Harold accidentally takes four doses of Viagra and runs amok in a brothel.
   Brooke has leukaemia and has 8 EPS to live.

When all the copies had been delivered, the plotters toasted. They were having fun. Even Sir Rex. 'Good stuff, Pentangeli.'
   'Thanks. Now what we need is a plant down on the floor tomorrow to listen – to see who's got a big mouth.'
   'Oh, I already thought of that. We got a plant.'
   'Who?'
   'You.'
   Stella smiled. 'Sir Rex, I'm not going to smoke out any spies being Stella Pentangeli.'
   He grinned and Stella felt the fear of the cornered rat when the cobra grins. 'Ah, but you won't be Stella Pentangeli. You'll be an actress called Danielle LeRoc and you have a day's stint on EP 294 of *The Young and The Naked* tomorrow morning. It's all arranged.'
   'Acting?'
   'Acting.'

*

In her years as a TV anchor and gossip reporter, Stella had never felt much more than a pleasant blast of fear and adrenaline just before the camera turned her way. The lens was a friend, the audience was one big jolly person who thought she was witty and adorable and hung on her every word. But anchoring was one thing. Public speaking and acting were a whole other terrible thing. Back in her glory days, she could make it through seminars and lectures on TVbiz by quaffing some extra Beefeater gins and never looking at the audience in case there, in the dark, were real persons with little un-jolly eyes all fixed on her.

As for TV and film acting ... forget about it. Once or twice some director would come up with the idea of having the TV reporter part played by Stella. 'A cameo,' they'd say. 'You'd be great,' they'd say.

But she would, invariably, be awful. Very quickly, directors stopped asking. In Actingbiz, even Beefeater couldn't save her from catastrophe.

*

Stella dreams the terror dream – the dream that every actor knows. She's on the set of a TV show or is it a theatre stage or maybe a public street and she doesn't know her lines and she's naked and everyone's laughing at her. She wakes up bathed with sweat a couple of times and has a Beefeater neat – only a small one – to calm her down. She goes back to sleep and has the same dream, the same sweats, the same sudden start to wakefulness, another Beefeater. Only a small one.

*

In the dirty alley behind Miss Bliss, Doorman #1 and Doorman #2 gaze fondly at the semi-conscious form of their own Smokin' Joe. He's slumped on a milk crate and they wonder what dreams he's dreaming. Has opium taken him to TerrorLand? Or to the Happiest Kingdom of Them All? Maybe both.

Mr Ma has told them, 'Make sure Joe's OK. Slip him some money now and then. Even some opium if he's hurting. Make sure he doesn't freeze in that alley. Make sure the local punks let him alone.'

From Mr Ma's demeanour, the doormen know there's some big action coming down soon in the Society – something nasty – and Mr Ma has decided he'll need all the luck he can get.

8.

THE YOUNG AND THE
NAKED ACTRESS

The next day, bright and early, 6 am, Stella was smuggled into Channel 3 and up to Sir Rex's office where she was bewigged, made up and dressed by an ancient lady loyal to Sir Rex. Stella was now a real-life non-existent actor named Danielle LeRoc who was to play a bit part in the hit supersoap, *The Young and The Naked*.

Her white hair was hidden under a thick red wig. She wore a becoming set of dark shell horn-rims with plain glass. Her wardrobe was 1980s slut – four-inch heels, hip-hugging mini, modified power pads on her coat, teensy shoulder bag. All in a vomitous electric green.

All this terror for 100 grand.

*

Director Peter Mountjoy – beatnik goatee, late 20s, English, South London imperious – waltzed onto the set with Frank String. String was craggily handsome, 70 but looked 55.

'Why, hel*lo*,' he said.

Mountjoy was delighted. 'And you are erm ...?'

'Danielle LeRoc,' Stella said in a choked voice.

'Danielle LeRoc. Of course.' He raised his voice to encompass cast and crew. 'Listen up, babies. Slight change to the script. One new scene, no biggie.'

He gestured towards Stella. 'This is Danielle Rock. She's to play the brief but coveted role of Frank's very secret and highly mysterious young mistress – or rather our naughty patriarch Harold Bellbird's very secret and highly mysterious young mistress.'

'And a very lovely mistress, too, if I may say so,' boomed Frank.

Everyone laughed dutifully.

Mountjoy: 'Well, from what I hear, you know all about young mistresses, Frank.'

Everyone laughed again.

String: 'Not these days, Petey. I'm an old man.'

Mountjoy: 'Never too old, Frank.'

The dutiful laughter was winding down rapidly. Mountjoy and String – pros to their bootstraps – moved the show along.

'Please make our new chum at home,' said Mountjoy. 'She's only here a day. What's your character's name?' Mountjoy asked.

Think!

'Erm . . . Star Choice,' Stella croaked.

'Star Choice?'

'Yes.' Stella's bowels churned liquid fear.

The director sighed sadly. 'Harold's been bonking – I kid you not, folks – a lady called Star Choice.'

A ripple of good-natured laughter from cast and crew.

'Miss Choice was, apparently, the reason Harold went amnesiac last month. Seems the sex was so good, the poor bastard lost his memory.'

'*That* I can believe,' said String gallantly.

So much panic blood was pounding in Stella's ears that she barely heard anything. She did, however, hear Mountjoy utter the words of death, 'OK, let's set it up.'

*

Danielle LeRoc didn't rate her own dressing room, since she had only a cameo. *But* she was a featured extra with dialogue, so her natural place wasn't really with those lepers of TVbiz, the atmosphere aka N/S aka non-speaking extras. But that was where she ended up. Which was what she and Zwikky had planned all along.

N/S extras are the people you see in the background of, say, the restaurant or the hospital. Their only job is to *be there and be quiet.* Thus, when in, say, the movie *Casablanca*, Rick and Elsa are emoting, the people around them who are engaged in drinking, talking, laughing etc are actually doing so in complete silence, since the sound of real talking or laughing would make editing the various takes of various angles of the scene impossible.

As the N/S and crew gossiped, Stella strained to hear. But the words 'Harold's getting married' or 'then finds the horse's head' never came up.

'My dear,' said Frank String, 'would you care for an espresso in my digs?'

'Me?'

'None other.'

Stella, from the corner of her eye, caught the nudges and winks.

This is String's modus operandi — chat up any halfway presentable newcomer, get her (or, probably, him) into the dressing room and hope for a quickie.

'Thank you, Mr String; that'd be lovely.'

He took her by the arm in his best olde-worlde manner and led the way.

*

Frank String is kissing Mae West and she's digging it. His lips brush her left ear. His left hand is making its way to her breast – he's hamming lust – and she's smiling Hollywood-happy into the camera. Even from this unflattering angle, Frank is a good-looking young man. A full head of dark curls, lashes a little too long, the groping hand tanned.

Frank is fighting unseen pirates. He wears artistically torn tight pants held up with a thick brown knife-dangling belt, knee-high boots, bandana, silver earring. His chest is tanned, buff, muscular. Smooth. His teeth flash white. He likes danger. Come and fight. Frank is a stud muffin and a half.

Frank and Jack Nicholson are at a party back when they were both in their early 40s. Drinks in hand. Relaxed. Brothers. You can feel the love.

An older Frank looks heavenward. He is dressed in the robes of a medieval Archbishop of Canterbury. His curls are greyer. His face craggier. His frame thicker. He looks great. He's every woman's dream lover, every girl's daddy, every man's vision of how to grow older with grace and horniness.

The photos – and a dozen more – are semi-indifferently scattered around the walls of his dressing room.

'What do you think, Danielle?'

'Oh my. This is embarrassing, Mr String.'

'What is, my dear?'

'Can I use your toilet?'

Sigh. 'But of course.'

*

Take two. Danielle emerges and it starts again.

'So, what do you think?'

'Oh my goodness,' trilled Danielle. 'Jack Nicholson. Russell Crowe. Sharon Stone.'

'Just the fond and fading memories of a fond and fading old actor,' said the great man modestly.

'Oh, you're not old, Mr String. You're immortal.'

String shrugged modestly but didn't deny it. He moved to a gleaming steel coffee machine and pressed a red button. Hiss and steam and rumble and fuss and *voila!* two espressos. 'Do you take sugar, my dear?'

Danielle blushed prettily. 'Oh dear, this is embarrassing again.'

Frank placed a hand on her shoulder. 'Tell Uncle Frank.'

'Well,' she said piteously, 'I love my coffee sweet but I have to watch the calories so I only ever have artificial sugar – you know, that FreeSweet.'

'We have it in the Extra's Mess. I'll fetch it, *immediatement.*'

'Oh no, Mr String. I'll . . .'

'Tut.' He held up a magisterial hand to silence her. 'FreeSweet it shall be.' He exited with a flourish. Stella immediately dived into the few pitiable drawers in the cheap dressing-room table and found a few empty pill bottles – nothing heavy – a couple of innocent looking letters, two twelve-packs of condoms *(Two? Gosh.)* and a lot of ancient dust balls. She slammed the drawers shut, then moved to the coat rack and quickly searched String's overcoat. No mini-cassettes or papers from the writers' department. The morning paper crossword page and his wallet.

His wallet.

She felt the guilt but did the job. She leant her back against the door and started rifling through. Not much cash, a lot of plastic, a few scribbled notes. One grabbed her attention. It was a plain white business card with the Channel 4 logo and 'Mo. 0555-6565' written on the back.

Mo? Mo Sherlock?

'Hello?' String barked from outside.

55

Stella butted the door closed with her rump, stuffed the business card back in the wallet and the wallet back into the overcoat.

String entered with packets of FreeSweet. 'What are you doing?' String's warm trust-me-I'll-be-gentle voice had hardened to suspicion.

0555-6565. 0555-6565. Remember it.

'Oh, Mr String, I'm so sorry. I was leaning against the door. I almost felt *faint* just thinking about all these people – these stars – you know. It's breathtaking.'

String was instantly mollified. His Wall of Fame had awed many a gal before. He stirred the FreeSweet into her coffee.

I've solved it already? Nah. I couldn't be this lucky. Life doesn't work that way.

'Why don't we sit on the couch? It's Italian. We could go over your lines or . . . something,' purred String.

They sat, sipped, put their coffees down. Stella pulled her script from her teensy shoulder bag. The script was the size of a small envelope.

'That's it?' said String.

'Oh Mr String, I only have two lines and I just can't remember them.' This was both IQ-70 Danielle and Stella Pentangeli talking.

'Read them for me,' said String in his best Actors' Studio Masterclass voice.

'Now?'

Sigh. 'Yes. Now.'

'OK. "Harold came to me in the night and it was as though our love was born anew for all time. In the morning when I awoke he was gone."'

String repeated it. '"Harold came to me in the night and it was as though our love was born anew for all time. In the morning when I awoke he was gone"?'

'See? There you go. You've only heard the lines once and you know them. I've been up all night trying to remember the damn things, and I can't.'

Real tears filled Danielle LeRoc's eyes. They were real because they were Stella's. In a few minutes she would be an actor in front of a camera playing a tart called Star Choice. Her brain had been turned into porridge. Frank put an avuncular hand on her knee.

'I'm here for you,' he said, looking into Danielle's eyes. His hand slid just a bit further up her poor distressed leg.

'Miss LeRoc, you're on now.' It was the PA's voice outside the door.

'Oh God.'

'You'll be fine, Danielle,' said Frank. 'Just fine. And we'll come back here and crack open some champagne when you're done.'

Stella and Danielle left Frank's dressing room and headed for their concurrent executions on Stage 2.

*

Ninety minutes later:

'Harold in the night was erm . . .' said Star aka Danielle aka Stella. 'Harold came in love. He . . . erm.'

'MISS LEROC! YOU'VE ONLY GOT TWO LINES!' Mountjoy's voice blared out of the speakers. His quasi-Oxford accent had curdled into South London crime crew. 'A five-year-old could do this.'

Stella agreed in every secret chamber of her soul. All she had to do was follow a simple plan –

1. *Enter the living room of Grandma Jones.*

2. *Say two sentences.* (Two sentences!) *'Harold came to me in the night and it was as though our love was born anew for all time.'* And, *'In the morning when I awoke he was gone.'*

57

3. Stand still and look worried till the director says cut.

Cast and crew were no longer her new pals – laughing, chummy, open. The female N/S mocked her behind their hands.

'I could have played Star Choice.'

'Me too. It might have been my big break.'

'Instead, they got this bozo.'

'This bimbo.'

The others, too, glared at her with differing mixtures of anger, scorn and pity. They'd pegged her for what she was – an actor's most deadly foe and ancient curse – a co-actor who couldn't act. A loathsome amateur thespian who, faced with TV cameras and vicious time pressures, broke out in flopsweat and could barely speak.

'I'm hungry.'

'Fire her.'

'Is there such a thing as a *reverse* lobotomy?'

Mountjoy appeared on the floor. He would coax this dumb bitch through her two lines, then take her outside, slit her throat and dump her in the losers' bin. In all his career, he'd never failed to get a scene and he wasn't going to start his failures now.

'Danielle, darling. Listen to Uncle Peter.'

Stella was Clarice Starling listening to Uncle Hannibal Lecter.

'Now, I know you're nervous.' His smile was friendly as cancer. 'But it's not like you're opening on Broadway in *Hamlet*. All you have to do is say: "Harold came to me in the night and it was as though our love was born anew for all time. In the morning when I awoke he was gone."'

Stella summoned her courage and gave it to Danielle. 'Harold was . . .'

'No. No. Harold CAME! Harold CAME! Holy Mother

of God! You can't even get out TWO BLEEDIN' WORDS without fucking up? What have you got under that wig? Brains? Or SHIT?'

Stella Pentangeli, showbiz detective – who had faced knives, guns, homicidal maniacs and more – broke down and cried. Mountjoy felt a twinge of guilt. Cast and crew glared at him.

Bully.

Limey creep.

Pommy bastard.

Stella snurfled in fear and shame. Mountjoy knew it was too late; that, not in a hundred years, would this chick be able to do this scene. She's gone. Miss LeRoc's mind has left the building. Then, BINGO! the great idea flew in the window.

'Gather round everyone. Slight change of plan. I've just decided that Star Choice is a deaf mute.'

He looked at Stella. The cast and crew looked at Stella. Stella, still snurfling, looked at the floor.

'I'm assuming, of course, that Miss LeRoc is capable of walking in a more-or-less-straight line without falling over.'

The new plan was –

1. *Enter the living room of Grandma Jones.*

2. *Hand Grandma a note.*

3. *Listen while Grandma reads out: 'My name is Star Choice. I am a deaf mute. Harold came to me in the night and it was as though our love was born anew for all time. In the morning when I awoke he was gone.'*

4. *Stand very still and try to look very worried till the director says cut.*

'Make up! Fix her face.'

*

This time, the scene went off without a hitch. Having no lines, Stella couldn't forget any. Ten minutes later, Danielle LeRoc's one and only scene, 29 miserable words, two sentences (*two sentences!*) was done.

'Thank you, my babies,' said the director from the roof booth. 'Miss LeRoc, get out of here before I murder you.'

Frank moved quickly towards her to claim his protégé and soothe her where she hurt. To his dismay, Norman appeared and took poor Miss LeRoc away.

*

Stella used Sir Rex's gold and marble bathroom to remove the wig, change her clothes, fix her face, bury her shame.

Rise above the humiliation. The mark of the warrior is to keep standing.

She re-entered the office and sat down with dignity.

'So, waddaya got, Pentangeli?'

'I didn't get much of a chance to eavesdrop.'

'I noticed.'

'You *noticed*?'

Clap took out a many-buttoned console and pushed a red button. The side wall opened like curtains to reveal a bank of a dozen screens. He pressed another button and they were looking at the *Young and Naked* set and the coffee corner. 'Yeah, I had all the mics and spare cameras open.'

'You *saw* me act?'

'Well, now ... I wouldn't call it *acting*. I gotta tell you, I haven't laughed so much since the first wife died.'

Stella snapped a glance at Norman, who was smirking.

Oh God. They both saw it. Rise above the humiliation. The mark of the warrior is to keep standing.

Clap pressed another button and the office was suddenly a hubbub of voices – some real, some acting. Two young N/S were kissing passionately in the smoking area. Clap pushed a button and all sound went down except the sound of the mouths churning with lust, groaning. He zoomed in and ogled.

'Great sound. Like we got the mic in their throats.'

'That's disgusting,' said Stella.

'You found something in String's pocket,' said Clap. 'What was it?'

'How do you know?'

Clap pressed a button. Four blank screens lit up to reveal the four dressing rooms.

'You wired the dressing rooms. That's a disgrace!' Stella yelled, furious. Clap looked up at her, genuinely puzzled. 'You can't spy on your own people like that.'

Clap looked at her. 'What d'you think *you're* doing?'

Which shut her up. Clap's sins and her sins were different in degree and method, not essence.

'What did you find in String's pocket?'

Stella was suddenly too dispirited to protest. She picked up an ornate titanium phone on Clap's desk and dialled 0555-6565. A recorded voice answered: 'Leave a message.' Stella hung up.

'Whose number was it?'

She pushed the re-dial button, handed Clap the phone and looked as he listened to the message. Clap put the phone down.

'Mo Sherlock. It's fucking Sherlock. That cocksucker String's got her fucking number. Her fucking secret spy number.' He doubled his volume. 'Norman.'

Norman entered immediately. 'Yes, sir.'

'Get String up here. Now.'

'Yessir.'

'Wait,' said Stella. Norman stopped and looked at his liege lord for instructions.

'Wait,' he barked.

'In fact, wait outside, Norman,' said Stella, delighting in this pocket of power.

'Yeah, Norman. Wait outside.'

With a look of hate at Stella, Norman stepped outside and closed the door.

If looks could kill . . .

'You're thinking of firing String, aren't you?'

'Damn right.'

'I'd advise you to wait.'

'Wait for what? That prick's Judased me.'

'We don't quite know that yet.'

'Sure we do.'

'Sir Rex, let the fake-outline scheme play out. Let's see what Mo Sherlock knows.'

'How do you plan to do that?'

'Easy,' said Stella. 'I'll ask her.'

Clap grinned at her. 'Pentangeli. You're something else.'

Yeah. But what?

9.

FOO, FA, FUN

Doormen #1 and #2 were proud of Smokin' Joe.

'He sure come up in de world, ole Joe.'

'He going to rise higher.'

Joe was slumped on a milk crate near the back door, sleeping or off with his sad pixies or dead, maybe. #1 shook him awake gently. Yellowed eyes, bleached bloodless skin. Eggs on snow.

#2 squatted next to him. 'Good news, Joe.'

Unsure smile from Joe. Crooked, dirty-tooth.

#1: 'Mr Ma say he don't want his good luck piece hangin' around da alley all de time.

#2: 'Mr Ma, he givin' you, just for today, free food, free dope and free pussy.'

#1: 'Smokin' Joe – dis is your life.'

They laughed. They picked Joe up and brought him in through the back door. Three young girls – Thai girls – were waiting. Maybe sisters. The eldest no more than 18.

#1: 'Hey bitches. Get him scrubbed up.'

'He smell,' said one girl.

#1 backhanded her. Not hard. Not soft. Just enough to make his point.

'Move.'

The girls took Smokin' Joe away, past a series of small jerry-built cubicles where the cheaper punters frolicked and into a separate area – the business end – suddenly glamorous. Faux marble. Discreet doors. Spa. Sauna. Erotic murals. This was where the high payers played.

#1: 'You plenty blessed guy, Joe. T'ree girls ta wash you. Miss Bliss charge big bucks for dat.'

#2: 'You Mr Ma's luck. He want you happy.'

Joe mumbled something but the doormen could tell Joe thought the whole thing – them, the whores, life – was just a dream.

*

First they strip his clothes. Smokin' Joe gibbers and jibbers and screams and grabs at his pipe and coat.

One of the girls places the now-cold pipe on a side table and says soothingly, 'See? You keep pipe, but clothes no good.'

Ng pretends not to hear but he is slipping the tiny lapel mic off the coat. He drops the coat and fondles his pipe. He slips the mic in the bowl and covers it with cold ash. One of the girls grabs up his stinky clothes and takes them away forever.

*

Operation Lincoln's main base was a battered old camping van parked round the corner from Miss Bliss. Specialists (Communication, IT) Constables Savage and Webster were crammed in with D.C. Lilly and state-of-the-art listening tech.

Savage breathed a sigh of relief. 'He recovered the mic.'

'Good *work*, Ng,' said Lilly.

'He's a clever bastard,' said Webster.

Operation Lincoln was still in business.

＊

The prettiest girl speaks to naked Smokin' Joe. 'Joe. I'm Fa.' She points first to the girl next to her, then to the third girl as she re-enters. 'This Foo. This Fun. We here for you. Understand? For you.' All three are dressed in tiny silk togas so tiny, so sheer that it's as though they too are naked.

Smokin' Joe nods and points. 'Foo. Fa. Fun.' The girls giggle and applaud as though he were the cleverest man in the world. Fa takes charge, leads Joe to the faux-marble shower cubicle, adjusts the water till it's just right and helps Joe in. She removes her toga and joins him. Naked, she is breathtaking – fine pale skin, small pink-tipped breasts, an inviting dark badge in the fork of her legs. She might be 18. She takes sweet-scented soap from a ledge and starts to clean the grease and filth that is Smokin' Joe. Foo places an elegant curved pipe in Joe's mouth. Ng knows he has no choice. He takes a small puff, mimes choking, hands it back.

'Have more,' says Foo.

'Enough,' said Joe.

'Mr Ma insi't. Insi't. Unnerstan'?'

'Unnerstan'.'

Just as Joe sucks up more smoke, the Dragon from the first hit floods his brain disguised as a single pure light of keen and eternal pleasure. Ng and Joe feel their jaws drop and their mouths open in wonder at the awful power of this joy. Foo strips off her toga and joins Joe and Fa. Foo – her hips and legs just a trifle thick – is luminous in her not-quite perfection. She starts to soap Joe's back. This is the most sensual moment of Joe's life – of Ng's life – of anyone *ever*'s life. He is erect. Fa soaps his phallus, his testicles. Foo soaps his back, his buttocks. Steam fills the cubicle. The

65

girls coo and whisper practiced obscenities as they rub. Ng comes in Foo's soapy hand and it seems to last forever.

'Good boy.'

'You strong.'

'Good boy.'

Fa turns off the water and they soap him all over. Lathered in soap, they lead him by the hand to the small sunken spa that Fun has readied. It's almost-not-quite-just-right scalding hot but the girls coax him in and, giggling, cooing, praising him, they make him stay till the soaking heat feels quite-just-right. Then, just like that, Ng is erect again. The girls giggle.

'Oh Joe.'

'You so strong.'

Fun takes off her toga. Of the three, she has the fullest breasts, the curviest hips. She's Stella in Asian miniature. All three join him in the spas, their hands rubbing away what's left of the soap. The spa jets come on at full pressure as Fun takes a mouthful of air and lowers her head onto Ng's greedy penis.

'It Fun's speciality. Underwater blowjob.'

Ng groans. He is beyond any sense of right or wrong. Is it Smokin' Joe or Investigator Ng who is drowning in pleasure at the beauty and power of these angels? Is it Joe or Ng who comes again in Fun's mouth? Whose face is it he sees as he comes? – with the white hair and the ferocious scowl and the shy smile? Does he groan Stella's name. No. Yes. Who knows?

One of the girls – Ng is beyond knowing which – shaves his stubbly head with care and trims his Fu Manchu. They dress him in a black silk kimono. One of them – Ng is beyond knowing – brings rice and noodles and pork and chicken cooked, Ng remembers, in the manner of Linlin. He picks at perfect food from Foo, Fa or Fun's perfect fingers as they lay on special cushions.

'You happy, Smokin' Joe?'

'Happy,' he croaks.

Fun or Foo or Fa fires up the pipe. Joe puffs. Ng, or is it Joe? – Ng is beyond knowing – is tired now. So tired. Is it Ng or Joe the girls massage as he drifts away to . . .

*

Even though Ng's lapel mic was under cold ashes in a pipe bowl, it continued to transmit. The Little Mic That Could.

'None of this leaves this van,' said Lilly. 'Ever. Are we clear?'

'Yes Ma'am,' said Savage.

'Absolutely,' said Webster.

But Lilly knew. This dam would not hold. The Night of Ng's Opium Binge and Underwater Blowjob would find its way into the legend of Ng some day.

*

Ng is shaken awake. Groggily, he is led out back still dressed in his silk kimono. Doorman #1 shoves him in the back of a car, then heads for Joe's Vice Valley room.

They know where I live, thinks Ng. They've been watching me.

#1 throws comatose Joe over one shoulder and hauls him up the rotting stairs of Famous Guest House. He heads straight for Joe's room.

They know my room number.

#1 has Joe's key and his pipe. He opens the door, eases Joe onto the bed, puts the pipe down. #2 moves to Joe and pats him affectionately on the cheek.

'Poor bastard Joe. He got nothing. But at least Mr Ma

67

send him to paradise for one night. Dat better than most of us get. See you tomorrow, poor bastard Joe.'

They leave, closing the door gently. Ng waits. He hears footsteps going down the stairs. He checks the pipe bowl. The mic is still there.

'I'm fine,' says Ng softly, urgently. 'Don't intercept the doormen. Repeat. Don't intercept the doormen. Come in.'

'Roger that. Come in.'

'Out.'

10.

MO

Stella wasn't surprised at the ease with which she got an interview with Maureen 'Mo' Sherlock, CEO of Channel 4.

She'll be curious about me. I would be.

Clap and Norman's melodramatic precautions meant there was only a small chance Mo knew Stella was Clap's spy. But – as in the city itself – walls have ears and whispers travel first class.

*

Stella's yellow VW fitted in well with most of the cars in the lot at Channel 4, aka the Poverty Network. Instead of the spacious grounds and offices of 3, the Channel 4 head office was on the first couple of floors of a low-rent low-rise in a Beacon Hill light-industrial park on the outskirts of the city. The head office was bad enough; but the Channel 4 studio was a further 20 kilometres away in the direction of even worse outskirts – the dreaded wastelands of Sunshine Hill.

Channel 4 was cheap and nasty. Channel 4 was ridiculous.

*

The lift was broken. Stella walked up to the second floor –
Mo's floor – which also housed the studio dining room. *Tout
le showbiz* was scandalised when Mo decreed the doors of
the dining room flung open to the public. But *tout le showbiz*
had to admit that the dining room was just about the only
Channel 4 making a profit.

Channel 4 was horrible.

*

The second floor smelt of hamburger with onion. *Yum.* It
boasted huge glossy shots of the stars of *Neighbourhood*,
local newsreaders, local ports commentators and many,
many photos of American cop and cowboy TV stars.

No wonder they're stealing from Rex Clap. All they have is
Neighbourhood *and a tuck shop.*

The receptionist was very impressed. 'I'm Ruth Reines.
I've heard so much about you, Miss Pentangeli. You're a
legend.'

Stella looked at Ruth Reines to see if she was joking.
She wasn't.

'Gee. Thanks.'

Ruth knocked on Mo Sherlock's office door.

'Come.'

Ruth opened the door and there was Mo in an office half
the size of Sir Rex's toilet. Minus the gold.

'Miss Pentangeli, come in. Thank you, Ruth.'

Ruth closed the door on them.

'Miss Sherlock. Pleasure to meet you at last.'

'Mo, please.'

She extended a friendly hand over her desk, shook hands,
motioned Stella to sit. 'Ruth will bring in coffee and cakes,
unless you'd like something else, Miss Pentangeli.'

'Stella. No. Thank you.'

They looked each other over.

Mo saw the 'legend'. The full figure, the glare of white hair. The legend looked pretty good.

Stella saw a woman in her early 40s, well-dressed, a carefully arranged mop of dyed red hair and a thin, cheery Irish face.

Mo was – compared to Stella – a newcomer. Even though Stella had been retired from TVbiz for a few years, she had lasted over a decade. Not easy. She had been a role model for three generations of TV women in that brief shiny moment when TVbiz welcomed intelligence and unconventional beauty.

Golden days, long gone.

'What can I do for you, Stella?'

'Well, Mo. It's just a puff piece about 4 for *The Pentangeli Papers*. I did Sir Rex and 3 and thought I'd give you guys equal time.'

'How is Clap these days?'

'Same old. Scary. Grumpy.'

'Give him my best when you see him.'

'I won't be seeing him for awhile.'

'You won't?' said Mo, all mock-puzzlement. 'I thought you were working for him.'

Here we go. She's heard something.

'I wouldn't work for him. Not if my life depended on it.'

'I thought you private eyes worked for anyone.'

'That's lawyers. Besides, what would Clap need with a private eye?'

Mo looked at Stella and smiled and Stella smiled right back.

'Well,' said Mo, 'I did hear around the traps that Clap's been accusing my channel of stealing ideas.'

'Yes,' said Stella carefully, 'I heard those rumours too. I figure it's because *Neighbourhood*'s doing so well.'

'We're nipping at *TY&TN*'s heels.'

'Good for you.'

They each played this game well. So well they both started when the receptionist said, 'Anything else?'

Ruth had poured the coffee and laid out the cakes.

Stella: 'Uh. No. Thanks.'

Mo: 'That's fine, Ruth.'

Ruth closed the door.

'Ruth's new. She's fabulous.'

New? Good.

'Speaking of new, Mo, what's new and interesting on *Neighbourhood*?'

'Same old.'

'Nothing spectacular?'

They locked eyes. All was dead silence except for a distant hum of a faulty air-conditioner somewhere far away. Finally –

'Nope.'

Silence. Finally –

'Well, this is going to be the shortest puff piece in internet history.'

They both faked a 'Hahahaha.'

'Come on, Mo,' Stella mock-begged, 'give me *something*.'

Mo shifted into autopilot. 'We at Channel 4 are immensely proud of *Neighbourhood*; as we are of all our shows. We've got several concepts we're workshopping now. A police drama, a quiz show, a late show.'

Workshopping. God, Channel 4 is pathetic.

Stella knew that, in TV talk, 'workshopping' was where a good idea landed on the desks of a few half-bright TV execs who umm-ed and ahh-ed and demographics-ed and brand-name-tested and tinkered and improved and pass-the-bucked till the idea lay gasping and bleeding to death and begging for a mercy killing. By then it was so hopelessly compromised and second-rate that no one in their right mind – especially the original TV workshopper – would even touch it.

'Sounds great.'

'We have very high hopes.'

Stella plastered a fake between-us-girls grin on her face. 'Between you, me and the lamp post, Elias Zwik and Sir Rex have a few surprises planned for *Naked*'s EP 300.'

Mo: 'Yeah?'

Stella: 'Yeah. I read some outlines.'

Mo: 'So? Spill.'

Stella: 'That wouldn't be ethical.'

Both: 'Hahahaha.'

Mo shifted topics: 'Elias Zwik – now there's an interesting guy.'

Stella: 'Yeah. The last non-suit suit in TVbiz.'

Mo: 'And quite a hunk if you like the grubby type.'

Stella: 'Who doesn't? Now and then.'

Mo: 'Renaissance feral.'

Both: 'Hahahaha.'

Stella slipped it in under the laughter. 'I was hoping to go on the *Neighbourhood* set, maybe chat with a few of the boys and girls.'

'Love to help you, Stella. But things are a bit ... delicate now at the studios.'

'I thought you said everything was same old.'

'Yes, but our same old is under wraps.'

'I'd never tell.'

Liar, liar, pants on fire.

Mo: 'Sorry.'

Stella: 'I never thought I'd meet an exec who didn't want maximum PR.'

Mo shrugged.

73

Stella pushed more. 'I just want to get a sense of the show.'

Mo shrugged again. 'Sorry.'

Stella's mouth went dry. *She's too insistent. She's already heard from the spy. The eagle has landed.*

'Never mind. So, how are things in the front office?'

'Fabulous.'

Both women wasted 20 minutes playing out the rest of the game, observing the grace and courtesies of good liars.

Finally –

'Great to see you, Stella.'

'You too, Mo.'

Ruth led Stella away. Once Mo's door was firmly shut,

Stella: 'Oh, do you have a business card if I need to follow up?'

Ruth: 'Absolutely.' She was pleased to be recognised as something other than the boss's diary and door-opener.

Stella: 'Excellent.'

*

Twenty minutes later, Stella pulled up at the main gates of Channel 4's run-down Sunshine Hill studios, her hair carefully wrapped in a scarf. Stella's hair was sometimes a hindrance to private-eying but it was also easy to hide and not scare the horses. She showed the guard her card.

'Drive right in, Miss Reines.'

'Thanks,' said Stella. 'Call me Ruth.'

*

Stella gazed at the five fragile sets that made up the fictional homes and corner shop of the fictional street in the fictional suburb of *Neighbourhood*'s Umina Beach. Two kids were in the shop set declaring eternal love. She was pretty. He was prettier.

Stella pondered the scene gloomily. A five-nights-a-week series is the lowest form of dramatic life. Her *TY&TN* ordeal had been bad enough but, after all, they were only making 47 minutes of TV a week. A strip show like *Neighbourhood* was making *110 minutes a week*. That's a full-bore feature-length movie every single week. 40 weeks a year. It is nothing less than an avalanche of spiked cannon balls, boiling oil and excrement which starts rolling after New Year and doesn't stop till November. If you fall, the avalanche will rip you to pieces, boil you alive and shit all over you. No time for nerves or weakness.

You got a hangover? Tough. Say the line.

You got leprosy? Tough. Say the line.

You're dead? Tough. Say the line.

Move it. Move it. Never mind the quality, fill the slot.

Even more frightening – in Stella's eyes at least – was the body count that shows like *Neighbourhood* left in their wake. She thought back to her first private-eye gig and the boy, Nelson J. Sharp, who'd peaked at 17 and spent the rest of his short life drugged, then insane, till he ended up dead. Most of the pretty young things in *Neighbourhood* currently boasting fan clubs and fat pay packets would meet their ends less dramatically but equally painfully. For they would . . .

fade away.

By 19 they would have grown too old to win hearts. They would be fired and then – when they needed to act – they'd realise they'd never learnt and didn't know how. They would go back to their suburbs and find work as what? barmen? checkout chicks? labourers? cleaners? The smart ones would have saved some money, then gone back to school or got married or did what real people do. They would treat their two years of fame as an excellent adventure to tell their children about in the years to come.

'Look! That was Daddy. Wasn't he handsome?'

'Look! That was Mummy. Wasn't she pretty?'

But there weren't many smart ones. Most would keep trying, trying, trying to grab the brass ring again. The tragic ones never recovered and were never forgiven by their real-life Neighbourhoods for rising so high and falling back to earth.

Whatever happened to Baby Jane?

Stella came back to earth and her mouth was dry. *I've been spotted.*

A floor manager came out of the dark. 'Can I help you?'

'I hope so. Ruth Reines, Miss Sherlock's personal assistant. I need to see all current plot outlines. It's rather urgent, I'm afraid.'

The floor manager spoke into his mic. 'A Miss Reines from Miss Sherlock's office. She wants to see the plot outlines.'

Stella heard it soft and clear through the manager's earphones. 'Why?'

'Why?' asked the floor manager.

'Because that's what Miss Sherlock wants.'

'Miss Sherlock sent her,' he said into his mic.

'Take her to Writers. Just get her the fuck off my set.'

'Right.' He smiled at Stella. 'The producer said to take you to Writers. This way please.'

*

The bowels of the old studio were even more depressing than the grim exterior. It had the same tired look as its city parent 20 kilometres away. Maybe Channel 4's interior decorators had created a new style for all their properties. Ancient Ennui. The halogen corridors had a certain *je ne sais quoi* that bespoke of being mopped only twice a week. The channel was so poor it was penny-pinching on cleaning contractors. Stella hurried to keep up with the floor manager. He looked back at her with a hurry-up-I'm-a-busy-man look. Stella scurried faster.

The sign on the opaque glass door was hand-lettered: WRITERS. The floor manager opened it, said 'Incoming from Beacon Hill!' then headed back to the studio. Stella shifted her stance from mild-mannered secretary to bitch from head office. She pushed the door open and strode in. There were four desks, one empty and all with elephantine desktop computers. Three writers glanced up incuriously. Two females, one male. Young, overworked, poor.

'Ruth Reines from Miss Sherlock's office. She wants a rundown on the latest *'hood* stories. As in now. Who's in charge?'

The younger of the two women stood. 'I guess that's me. Louie is off sick.'

'Louie?' said Stella.

A look of vague unease came over the woman. 'Louie Bateman. The head writer.'

She's wondering why, if I'm such a big shot, I don't know this Louie character. Quick!

'You mean *Mr* Bateman,' she snapped.

'Yes Ma'am.'

Bingo!

'What's your name?' said Stella.

'Joan,' said Joan.

Stella noted with satisfaction that the other two writers were busily heads-downing, out of the line of bitch fire. *Neighbourhood*, she could see, was a shitty job. But it was a job. In TVbiz, a job is a job is a job. In TVbiz, writers *do* grow on trees. In TVbiz, there's always someone more talented and they're knocking on the door.

Stella smiled at Joan with the patience of Job.

'Joan?'

'Yes Ma'am?'

'Would you mind getting me the goddam rundowns sometime before Christmas?'

Joan snapped to, leapt to her feet, rummaged through a battered filing cabinet and emerged victorious. 'Ah. Here we are,' she said brightly, hoping her mood might infect the grumpy cow. But no, the cow was now snapping her fingers impatiently. Gimme, gimme.

'We could have faxed this, Miss Reines. Or emailed it. Or ...'

Keep pushing. Keep them off guard. Confuse. Distract.

'Joan, if Miss Sherlock or I had wanted it faxed or emailed, we would have told you, wouldn't we?'

'Yes Ma'am.'

Snap. Snap. Gimme, gimme. Joan handed Stella the papers. She ran her eyes down two pages of synopses and ...

there it was.

NEIGHBOURHOOD: *FORWARD PLANNING.*

Old Mr Shelley marries a young nurse.

Young Sam's new horse is found dead. (Maybe horse head found in gym.)

No doubt about it. Just 24 hours back, they had concocted fake storylines for *TY&TN* and given them to the actors only –

1. *Harold Bellbird, who has recovered his memory, marries the very young nurse, Casey, who helped him in the nuthouse.*
2. *Brooke finds her beloved new horse, Thunder, has been decapitated and the head left in her school locker.*

Now there were young nurses marrying old fellas all over the place; and a glut of horses' heads as well.

The spy is one of the actors.

'I'll take that, thank you.'

Stella's heart THUMPED! She turned to Mo Sherlock glaring at her, the guard from the gate at her side – both looked murderously serious. Without taking her eyes off Stella, Mo said, 'Someone call the police.'

'You heard her. Someone call the police,' said the guard, trying to atone for his earlier sin of letting this ... this liar onto the grounds.

All three writers grabbed their phones and dialled at once. Stella thought – not for the first time – of Winston Churchill's comment about Germans: they were either at your throat or at your feet. In her experience, the TVbiz ladder was firmly planted in the earth of a quasi Third Reich.

'If I were you, I wouldn't bring the police in,' said Stella with more confidence than she felt.

'Why not?' said Mo, all confidence. 'You've trespassed and committed industrial espionage.'

'That's true,' said Stella.

Joan had won the get-the-police race. 'Sunshine Hill Police Station?'

'If I were you, I'd get Joan to hang up.'

'Hello. Yes. I'd like to report an attempted burglary,' said Joan.

'I've got two words for you, Mo: Rex Clap.'

'So?'

'That's who I'm working with. Do you really want to accuse Sir Rex of being a spy and a burglar?'

Mo took a micro-second to ponder. 'Oh, for Chrissakes, Joan, hang up.'

'Excuse me?' said Joan.

'Hang up!'

'You heard the lady. Hang up!' said the guard.

Joan put down the phone.

'Escort Miss Pentangeli out,' said Mo to the guard.

'Yes Ma'am.'

The guard grabbed her arm roughly. Stella didn't even think about it. She slammed her high heel down on the guard's foot and he screamed and hopped round the room as Stella waved bye-bye.

'I'll let myself out, thanks.'

*

When she got to her VW, the adrenaline kicked in and she had to wait a few minutes before her hands stopped shaking enough for her to drive.

11.

NIGHT OF THE RUSSIANS

Cross's slicing and dicing of the Russians was one of those pieces of luck that had often come Mr Ma's way. He had decided a while ago that the Russians would have to go. Now was perfect.

Since the collapse of the USSR, Russian – or, rather, ex-Soviet – crime gangs had spread to North and South America and Western Europe. Australia, and this city, especially, had been spared partly through geography and luck and partly, because the Docs and Ma's were very good at policing foreign crime. In his more frivolous moments, Ng often thought that if the crime gangs were police support units, the city would be the safest in the world.

There were ten Russians in all, bound by Georgian blood, marriage and a fierce desire to carve out a tiny empire. If they could manage to survive, they would grow. If they grew, sooner or later the Australian and the Chinaman would agree to accept tribute and let their empire thrive. Now they'd been humiliated by this ex-policeman, they'd be needing quick vengeance.

*

Fuk Chin Society assassins burst into the Russians' HQ at a few minutes after midnight. HQ was a big word for a small-time inner-suburban wreckers' yard. Two of the Russians lived in a shack adjoining the yard office. Three more lived in an illegal caravan hidden behind the car wrecks. The other five were scattered in outer-suburban houses or inner-city apartments with their families.

The Russians had just finished their meeting –

'This fat pig with the hooks for hand must suffer and die.'

'Publicly.'

'Publicly.'

'Agreed?'

'Agreed.' All of them knew it was risky to kill an ex-policeman, but he had stupidly left them no choice –

CRASH!

It was stereo shootout sound. The front door burst open just as the side window shattered glass all over them. Four Fuk Chin with SA80s came through the door, one Fuk Chin with a Glock stayed at the window to shoot and cover. All the Russians were dead within 30 seconds. The Fuk Chin used machetes on two of them and left a few body parts scattered round *pour encourager les autres*. They packed what was left of their corpses into the 'Happy Farm Meat' van *en route* to Doc's boatshed and butchering crew.

*

The Premier's fund-raiser at Parliament House, in the Strangers' Dining Room, was a glittering affair. *Tout le showbiz*, including Frank String, media supremos – Sir Rex Clap, Mo Sherlock, Elias Zwik, the big-end-of-town boys and plain party faithful, were there to pay obeisance to the Great Man. TV cameras and press photogs were allowed in for one half-hour exactly. Journos were allowed a few easy questions. Then they were turfed out. Stella didn't bother to go; Terry found real-world night too terrifying. They both agreed Terry should emulate your typical society journo and just make something up. He and Stella were there in cyber-spirit.

*

SHOWBIZ! SHOWBIZ! SHOWBIZ! ONLINE!
THE PENTANGELI PAPERS ***EXCLUSIVE***!
OUR BETTERS AT PLAY
by Terry Dear
The Premier's annual fund-raising bash. God A' mighty!
Is there anything more puke-inducing, more mind-destroying,
more suicidal-thoughts-inducing than the sight and sound
of the Government wagging its collective arse and
howling in joyful song and dance?
Our very own Stella Pentangeli was there in a daringly low-cut
black silk number and seemed the very belle of the ball.
She laughed gaily at the many very funny jokes
essayed by Sir Rex Clap and . . .

*

Once the press were herded out, modest Doc Mortaferi, the well-known philanthropist and businessman, entered from a side room to join the festivities. The big end of towners saw Doc as an amusingly naughty equal; their wives and girlfriends found him exotic.

'Great tan.'

'He loves the sea.'

'Nice bottom.'

'Very nice.'

'I hear he has people *killed*.'

'Well, he can start with this caterer.'

83

'Hahahaha.'

The Premier had no qualms about socialising with Doc, but he took sensible precautions. For instance, he waited till a particularly loud dance session, before taking Doc aside and, with extra volume in his patrician voice, bawling, 'I must say, Mr Mortaferi, how worried I was getting about all these Russian mobsters crawling out of the woodwork.'

'Me too, Mr Premier.'

Doc had never figured out exactly how much the Premier knew about things, or how many of his colleagues Doc now owned. Sexy young women, gay boys, gambling, drugs – Doc supplied the best at the best prices, then never failed to come and collect.

'This is a clean town, a fine city,' the Premier yelled firmly. 'I'd hate those kind of thugs to get a foothold.'

'I wouldn't worry too much, Mr Premier! Aussies would make mincemeat out of em!'

The Premier winked. 'Or shark meat, eh?'

The loud music ended so the Premier left it at that and wandered away. Doc was – strangely, paradoxically – mortified. The Premier knew a lot – perhaps *the* lot. It was a fucking disgusting way to run a democratic government.

The band played on. The men's faces grew redder, the women grew bolder.

'Mr Mortaferi, you're going to think me a dreadful woman, but I was telling my friend Jane here that you and she and I should get the Premier to secure the parliamentary swimming pool for us. I hear he's hung like a stallion.'

Jane giggled. 'Skinny-dipping. Jiggy-jig. You name it. I've got some killer cocaine – mboké. It'll cure what ails you.'

But Doc, inconsolable, just gazed at them, then turned and wandered away. For a few hours, as the cages settled on the bottom of the sea floor, and the creatures of the deep started sniffing round the bodies, and the song and laughter echoed round the Strangers' Dining Room, Doc was a dismayed Diogenes stalking through the marketplace of this sad and pitiless world, lantern lit, looking for an honest man and finding no one home except drugged and drunken rich girls.

*

Ma believed in deniability too. The night of the Premier's fundraiser, he had organised an ostentatious banquet in Chinatown's finest restaurant, Rising Sun, for a dozen or so of his closest friends, all Chinese. Smokin' Joe sat at the table on Ma's right. King Ma and his Fool. Joe grinned. Joe looked out of place. Ma got drunk and boisterous.

Just after 1 am, Ng saw a Fuk Chin lieutenant enter and whisper in Ma's ear, 'Russian package delivered.'

The message seemed to be very good news for Ma. He said, 'Someone give Joe a present. I love Joe. He's my luck.' One of the young men slid a ball of top-grade opium across the table.

'Here you are, Joe,' said the young man.

'Don't smoke all that at once, Joe,' said Ma.

But Joe was already off to the gents. The guests burst into laughter. Joe's need and desperation was funny.

'Look at him go.'

'Run, Joe, run.'

Ma beamed round the table, happy and at peace with his world. Mr Ma giveth and Mr Ma taketh away; blessed be the name of Mr Ma. All that he required was the love and respect that was his due. And he was getting both in abundance.

85

*

Ng picked a stall with a view of the door. He lit a piece of the crumbly grey magic – enough to stink up the cubicle – and spoke quietly into his lapel.

'Is there any news about Ma and Russians? Come in.'

'We have an unsourced report of Russian mobsters killed at Hellbow Park. Come in.'

'Ma is using Mortaferi's boatshed. There will be bodies there now. Come in.'

'I can't authorise a raid based on a guess. Come in.'

'Understood,' said Ng. 'Contact Rodney Cross on his mobile. He's to go to Mortaferi's with a camera. Come in.'

'Can't do that. Cross is a civilian. Come in.'

'Do it. Please.'

'Ng. (pause) Ng?'

No answer.

*

They were about to 'fish old Joe out of the toilet bowl' when he floated into the room, stoned and blissful. The whole table roared with laughter. The Rising Sun dinner was proving a huge success.

12.

PENTANGELI AND
ASSOCIATES

1.10 am. Cross's snores pierced Stella's bedroom wall and rubbed her nerves just a little rawer.

I'll kill him.

Cross had been asleep on the living-room couch for less than two hours yet. He was one of those snurfle-gurgle-and-gaspers who erupt briefly but loudly when you least expect it, then stay quiet and wait.

I'll kill him, no jury would vote to convict.

Earlier that evening he had arrived with take-away curry for two and two six-packs for one.

'Cross,' she'd said with the mock severity he always brought out in her, 'you don't just drop in unannounced. I might have been entertaining.'

'Are you?'

'No.'

'You like curry?'

'Yes.'

He dangled the package from his hooks. 'It's from The Delhi Belly. It's the best in town.'

She faked a pout, heaved a sigh and let him in. The Delhi Belly *was* the best in town. They ate and drank and it was good. This new, improved Cross was easygoing and talkative and *loving* his new high profile.

'Listen, Stells. You can mention me in your online rag any time you want. One little mention and I'm getting more pussy than Mick Jagger.'

'I'm glad *The Pentangeli Papers* were able to pimp for you.'

'Oo boy. Me too.'

He bragged. She scoffed. She talked. He listened. She talked about the Channel 3 gig. She talked about Ng. He talked about Ng. Although they tried, neither could hide they were talking about – no other word – their love for him. They drank. They laughed. Cross said Stella needed a partner in her 'agency'. Stella disagreed. Cross spoke for the affirmative case, Stella for the negative. The beer ran out. Cross switched to Stella's Beefeater gin. They talked about the delicate difference between solitary and . . .

and lonely.

Finally, around midnight, Cross said, 'Stells. Can I grab a few z's on the sofa? I'm too pissed to drive.'

'OK.'

'OK.'

Stella went to bed but sleep wouldn't come. She felt like crying.

Too many gins. Mother's ruin.

She missed men. She missed Ng.

I won't kill Cross. Even he's better than . . .

lonely.

Stella's mobile beeped loudly. She grabbed for it like a drowning man grabs a lifesaver. Nothing. Cross's mobile.

'Cross,' he said, instantly awake. 'Yeah? (pause) Right. (long pause) Yeah.' He hung up.

Stella entered, wrapping herself in a robe. 'Was that Ng?'

'Nah. It's some chick he's working with.'

Bristle. 'He's working with a woman?'

'Yeah. Sounded hot, too. She said Investigator Ng wants us out at Doc Mortaferi's place like ten minutes ago.'

'Why?'

'To take photos.'

'Of what?'

'Investigator Ng's got a hunch that Doc's boys are doing dump jobs in the ocean tonight.'

'The boatshed?'

Cross was surprised. 'You know about the boatshed?'

'Ng told me.'

Cross was putting on his coat and getting his street face ready. 'You got a camera I can borrow?'

'I'm coming with you.'

'No way.'

'Ng needs help.'

'No, Stells. Investigator Ng needs *my* help. Not a . . .'

'Not a dumb chick? Is that it?'

Cross opened his mouth. Closed it again. Stella moved closer and crooned. 'Come on, Cross. It's like a road test for Stella Pentangeli and Associates.'

'*Associates*? I'm gonna be an *associate*?'

'Maybe.'

'Let's go,' said Cross.

Stella dived into her bedroom and – to Cross's delight – he caught a big juicy glimpse of her bod as she changed into an old track suit. Oh that wondrous Italian arse. Oh those tits. Oh Lucky Ng.

Stella was ready. She grabbed her digital camera, exited her bedroom, moved into his face. 'Let's go.'

'Yes, boss.'

*

Stella gunned her 80s VW towards Bayside Bay.

'Tell me, Cross.'

'What's that?'

'Why hasn't Ng closed down the boatshed?'

Cross pondered. Interesting question. 'I guess . . . too many people are sorta glad it's there.'

'Like who?'

'The brass and the pollies for one.

'That's never stopped Ng before.'

Cross looked at her, then looked off at the night speeding by. 'I think the Investigator's sorta glad it's there, too.'

Shock crossed Stella's face. 'Are you kidding me? Ng hates murder worse than . . .' she paused and added lamely, '. . . death.'

'Better ten bad guys should be sliced up in Doc's boatshed than that one good guy should be gunned down in the streets.'

'So you let a thug like Doc Mortaferi be judge and executioner of bad guys?'

He looked at her like she was the thickest student in his crime academy. 'Sure. Yeah. Sometimes. Why not?'

'That's the job of the legal system. The justice system.'

Cross snorted. 'The people who get justice are people who can pay for it or know where the system's bodies are buried.'

'Bullshit.'

Cross grinned at her. 'Try walking into a courtroom sometime without a few hundred thou to spend.'

Stella opened her mouth, then closed it again. *When did I become such a big fan of pollies and judges?*

'Plus, you gotta remember, if anyone killed a good guy in Doc's shed, Ng wouldn't have to go after them. Doc would kill em, himself.'

'Why?'

'Doc has a code he lives by.'

'Like you and Ng.'

Cross beamed. *'Now* you're getting it.'

*

Stella and Cross staked themselves out on a sandhill 50 metres down from the Mortaferi mansion. The wind was still, the water black, the sand gritty.

Their timing was lucky – so good that Stella and Cross saw the cruiser, 'Doc's Pride', lowered by pulley chains to the metal slipway, then edged out to sea. On board, covered with tarpaulins, was a huge square pile of something.

Stella snapped away.

'Jesus,' said Cross.

'What? What's under the tarpaulins?'

'They gotta be stiffs.'

'Bodies?'

The cruiser powered up and headed away. 'I figure he's got eight cages under the tarp. Eight, maybe ten bodies.'

'Ten?'

'Yep. A while back, me and some MVC&IP mates went to an abattoir and had them carve up a few hundred kilos worth of cow. We figured out the best way to pack it.' Cross warmed to his theme. 'You need just under one square metre per cage per corpse if you do it right; and Mortaferi's crew do things right.'

'Gee. Thanks for sharing that.'

A Treatise on The Art of Efficient Corpse Dismemberment and Dispersement, by R. Cross.

A gust of wind blew sand in her mouth and she spat it out. The same gust lifted the tarpaulin clear off its cargo. Stacked neatly, two cages high and four cages wide, were small-meshed large-scale battery-hen cages stuffed with meat which was once men. It was many seconds before the crew lashed it back. Stella kept capturing the evidence, refusing to acknowledge what she was seeing.

'Maybe eleven bodies,' said Cross.

The ghost ship cruised out into the black.

*

One by one, Stella ran the pictures through her laptop. They were all useless as any kind of evidence – except to identify the boat as 'Doc's Pride'. Some men on a night-time boat cruise. No big deal. Except for the one photo which was like a preview of hell.

Eight cages.

In the foreground of one cage, a half-face with one eye open, looking puzzled.

A hand.

A half-foot.

A foot.

Eight cages of extra-meaty, double-crunchy shark food.

A sign on the boat's side: 'OC'S PRI'.

'We got him,' said Cross.

'What do we do now?'

'Download it onto to your laptop. Hide the camera, hide the laptop. Wait till Ng surfaces.'

'Good thinking.'

'That's what associates are for, boss.'

13.

NOSFERATU

Stella drove her VW into Channel 3's lot. There was no
need for disguises this time.

She had woken from a nightmare in which she was chained
to the bottom of the ocean, surrounded by cages of laughing
lobsters who nipped at her eyes. During her quick shower
to the funereal sound of Cross's snores, during her drive to
Channel 3, she kept alternating between brief snatches of
mirthless giggles and an urge to burst into tears. Steering
with her knees, she popped half a TranQuax and hoped it
would kick in before she faced Clap and Zwikky.

*

'From the evidence at Channel 4 Writers, there's no doubt
Mo Sherlock's info came from your actors' fake storylines.'

'String,' said Clap quietly.

'We don't know that, Sir Rex.'

'He had Sherlock's number in his wallet.'

'There are a dozen legit reasons why he would. It could
be any of the actors or crew.'

'It was String,' said Zwikky suddenly.

'How do you know?'

Zwikky looked at Stella, weighing up whether to divulge or not. He looked at Sir Rex who shrugged.

'I got a call last night from a friend. The friend works in a bank where Mo Sherlock has her account. Three weeks ago, Sherlock wrote String a cheque for ten grand.'

Ouch.

'He faxed me a copy of it.'

There it was on Clap's desk. A cheque from the enemy to the eldest and most beloved member of Sir Rex's Channel 3 family. 'If he'd asked me,' said Clap. 'I'd have given him *ten*, hell, *fifty* grand. I loved the man. The prick.'

'Maybe you can hush it up,' said Stella. 'That'd be better all round.'

Clap stared at Stella with contempt. Then, 'Norman!'

Norman was instantly there.

'I want security to throw Frank String off my property.'

'Frank String?'

'Now.'

'Yessir.'

He was halfway out the door when Zwikky stopped him with a simple, 'No.'

Norman looked at his master who looked at Zwikky. 'Sir Rex, as a favour to me, let me do it. Let's give the man a little dignity.'

'Fuck his dignity.'

'Please.'

'No.'

'Hear me out,' said Zwikky. 'Please.'

'What?'

'I used to see Frank String at the movies when I was a kid. Remember how *honoured* we were when he signed with us – remember? He gave the show *class*. Please. Let's show some class, too.'

The big bad angel and the very tiny good angel in Clap's soul wrestled for a few moments. 'OK. But I still want him out. Now. I'll get PR to put out the usual "creative differences" crap.'

'Thanks,' said Zwikky. 'I owe you.'

Sir Rex shrugged that off. 'Norman. Get PR up here. Get the *Naked* director – Mountbatten – up here.'

'Mountjoy, Sir Rex.'

'Whatever. And cut a cheque for Pentangeli. A hundred thousand.'

'Dollars?'

'No, you moron. Beans.'

'A hundred thousand dollars. Yessir.'

The TranQuax hit. An Angela Drumm song flashed in Stella's brain.

Judas, Judas, flirty, flirty.
Thought the gig was only thirty.
I told the priests that you got plans.
Told the priests you want a grand.

*

Stella sat in her car outside the Channel.

I ratted him out.

The word had spread. A few Channel 3 employees gathered at the main door and peered through the second-storey windows.

Zwikky would have begged Frank to not make a fuss, to walk away. Keep up appearances in front of the 'family'.

Zwikky and Frank String – head high and all smiling teeth – exited the main doors.

The show must go on.

Zwikky led the old man over to the VW, and leant in.

More employees appeared at the windows.

95

Zwikky loaded String into the back seat and climbed in with him.

'Drive. Now,' said Zwikky.

He wants to help. To hold Frank's hand. To be his shoulder. Zwikky's the one showing class.

*

Stella drove them to Frank's notorious *Nosferatu* mansion. It took both Zwikky and Stella to ease Frank out of the car. He had aged a thousand years in an hour.

*

Creaky gate. Just room enough for the VW next to the front porch of *Nosferatu*. Barred windows. Graffiti. String hadn't said a word the whole trip. He spoke now.

'Come in, come in.'

But it wasn't an invitation, it was a plea. Don't leave me here. Not tonight.

'Under the brick.' And, sure enough, in the middle of the most crime-ridden part of the city, there was the key to the decaying mansion right next to the front door.

*

In the 50s, he'd bought *Keene House*, an 1800s' two-acre, ten-bedroom, three-bathroom, spires-towers-gardens-pool-tennis-courts mansion in fashionable Viceroy Valley. String renamed it *Nosferatu*, the undead.

'Just one of my little jokes,' he dead-panned.

Nosferatu became the antipodean *Garden of Allah* or Court of the Sun King. Two and three day parties. Buckets of punch. Bowls of mboké cocaine. Forests of weed.

Uppers. Downers. Nude waitresses. Nude waiters. 'Drugs? Liquor? Me?' they'd say.

The city was proud of its native son. So much Hollywood glamour. *Here.* From the start, police and pollies were too busy partying to bust him.

The public adored him.

'That Frank. So naughty.'

'I hear if it moves, he roots it. That Frank.'

'That Frank. He's a *star.*'

One decade. Another. The fame started peeling and cracking. Only Frank's spending remained constant. He spent less and less time in front of movie cameras and more and more time on TV. *Dean Martin's Celebrity Roast, Hawaii 5-0, Mod Squad, The Homicide Boys.* Then *Hollywood Squares, Tic-Tac-Toe, Celebrity Squares, Blanketty-Blank.* Then, suddenly ... nothing.

He sold off an antique piece here and a quarter acre there, till all that was left was the crumbly mansion.

In many people's secret hearts, they never really believed Frank's Hollywood tales. He'd been spinning them for decades. But Frank knew. He was there. It was true. Errol and Burt and Ava and Frank and Gregory Peck and Fred Astaire and Judy. All true. They'd danced in the ballroom downstairs; they'd slept in these very rooms. True. All true.

*

Inside. The top two floors of the mansion were sealed off. Frank led them through a huge ballroom with rot round the sides.

Ten, 20, 30 years ago this mausoleum would have been packed with laughter and decadence. Now not even ghosts live here.

String's main home was a tiny bedroom with a cluttered kitchen and tiny parlour. From the smell, he seemed to live on baked beans and champagne.

'I ... seem to ... be out of ... erm ... liquor,' said Frank.

The sentence took forever to finish. He sat down heavily at the kitchen table, a world hanging on his shoulders.

Zwikky spoke up, gently. 'Listen, Frank. If it's not too rude of me, I'll just nip out and buy a few bottles of bubbly.'

'Be rude as you like, dear boy.'

'And, Zwikky . . . maybe some brandy,' said Stella.

Zwikky looked at her and nodded. He'd gotten her message: *String's in some sort of shock.*

'Brandy it is.' And he was gone.

Well, well, Elias Zwik. I'm finding you more impressive by the minute. Almost Ngian.

She recoiled at her lack of loyalty.

Silence. Then String seemed to remember she was there. He smiled at her. 'I got fired today.'

Stella nodded. 'I know.'

He peered closer. 'I remember you, my dear.' He pondered. 'Yes. Danielle. You had different hair. You couldn't remember your lines. The director was very rude to you.'

'That's right.'

'I despise rudeness.'

'Thank you.'

He peered closer. 'Strange. Before you were Danielle, you were someone else. On TV. S for something.'

'Yes. My real name's Stella Pentangeli.'

'Ah yes, of course.' Puzzled. 'How many names do you have, my dear?'

Stella blushed. Then, too complicated for him, String dropped the topic. Then he stared around the grubby little room as if he'd forgotten where he was for a moment. Then, 'I got fired today.'

'I know. You said.'

'Never been fired before. Not nice.'

Stella had to know. 'Why did you do it, Mr String?'

'Frank, please.'

'Why did you do it, Frank? Was it for money?'

Frank looked at her, puzzled. 'Do what, dear lady?'

'Betray Sir Rex.'

He looked at her, more puzzled. 'Betray Sir Rex? My dear, I didn't. I never would.'

OK. Live the lie. You're the actor.

Zwikky returned with a carton – a dozen champagnes, cognac, Beefeater.

'No, no,' said Frank. 'This is too much.'

'They were on special,' said Zwikky. 'Stella, pour the man a brandy, will you?' She poured. Zwikky popped. Grubby glasses.

'Cheers.'

'Cheers.'

'Happy days.'

String downed the brandy in one gulp and thrust his arm out for another. Stella poured. This time String sipped.

'They tell me,' he said, 'that I sold secrets about my show. I didn't. That's unthinkable. That's against everything I hold sacred.' He thought about it and was sure. 'You have honour or you haven't. If you haven't, life is meaningless.'

He's cast himself as the innocent man and there's no one to call 'Cut!'

Mood swing. He regaled them with thousand-times-told tales of the West End and Broadway and Hollywood. He told the most famous String story of all. Thirty years ago, he was making a tits-swords-and-sandals epic in Spain. One Monday morning he didn't arrive onset. A virginal young Spanish second PA was sent to his villa to fetch him. She knocked on the front door, then came round the back, to see a dazed String inside; he was tied naked to a chair. Alarmed, she broke in and untied him.

'Oh, my dear girl,' he said. 'What a FABULOUS weekend I've had.'

By midnight, he started to drift off. Zwikky placed him gently on the bed, removed his shoes and tucked him in tight. 'We'll never see his like again,' he murmured.

Amen.

Zwikky leant down and kissed the old man gently on the forehead.

*

Stella dropped Zwikky off at his Lower Lofty Range log cabin.

'Come inside,' he said.

*

It was a log cabin in the sense that it was made of logs.

'It's got four bedrooms, two bathrooms, spa, sauna and a cleaner and gardener who pop in to keep things nice. *Bourgeois*, huh?'

'Jesus,' said Stella. 'How the hell do you pay for all this?'

'I don't,' said Zwikky. 'I rent it from Sir Rex. One dollar a year.'

'That old guy really loves you, doesn't he?'

'Yeah.' Then he was embarrassed. 'Coffee?'

'Erm . . . no thanks.'

'How about a long, lingering kiss in the nude?'

'What?'

'Oh. Suppose a fuck's out of the question?'

She burst into surprised laughter. 'That's an oldie, Mr Zwik.'

'But a goodie, Miss Five Angels.'

They both knew he was joking but wasn't; both knew she was tempted; both knew he'd ask again; both knew she'd probably say yes.

*

SHOWBIZ! SHOWBIZ! SHOWBIZ! ONLINE!
THE PENTANGELI PAPERS ***EXCLUSIVE***!
FRANK STRING LEAVES TY&TN.
Frank String has left his popular role as patriarch Harold
Bellbird in TY&TN *despite the lustre his acting*
and personality added to the hit soap.
Sir Rex Clap, head of the Channel 3 network, said that 'he
was personally saddened to see the great man go.
Frank wants to pursue other interests.
Channel 3 is a family and I would never hold a member
of the family back. God bless him.'
Mr String is believed to be considering several movie
and commercial offers. He . . .

14.

COPS BAR

On his way home after spying on Doc Mortaferi's death cruise, Cross knew he wouldn't be sleeping for a while. He felt the old pleasant buzz of adrenalin subsiding, of a job well done. He knew he'd never sleep, so he stopped off at one of his old police stomping grounds – a bar in Vice Valley. It had no official name; it was always the Cops Bar – small, stinky and a magnet for police just finishing a shift. Only a few selected crooks were allowed in but the door was wide open for 'copsuckers' – the traditional city name for girls, women and discreet gents who liked the breed.

Cross seldom got drunk these days. He'd gotten to like waking up feeling human. He planned to have just one or two but both police and copsuckers had heard about the already-legendary Day of the Russians and they all wanted to buy him a drink and shake his hand or something more personal and Cross didn't want to offend anyone by refusing and soon the one or two turned into five or six and more and when old comrades from MVC&IP rocked in, Cross was blitzed and boasting about how he and Stella Pentangeli were associates and they had just fucked up Ma and his

Fuk Chins and Doc big time and had the photos of the death boat to prove it.

'In living colour. I mean dead.'

They laughed. They all agreed they missed Cross in MVC&IP.

'You're the king, Cross.'

'Three cheers.'

'Buy the big man a drink.'

One of the Valley rats – a small-time dealer/junkie – stepped outside to make a call to a friend of a friend who knew someone who knew Mr Ma.

15.

INCONTINENCE PADS

CONFIDENTIAL.
FINAL DRAFT – YOUNGMAN'S INCONTINENCE PADS
COPY 09. MR STRING

<u>1. EXT BEACH</u>   <u>DAWN</u>

MAN (MR STRING) LOOKS OUT OVER AN EXPANSE
OF SEA AS THE SUN RISES.

> **MAN (VOICE OVER)**
> Some things in life are beautiful . . .

CUT TO:

<u>2. EXT GOLF COURSE</u>   <u>DAY</u>

MAN HITS A FABULOUS TEE-OFF SHOT.

> **MAN (VO CONT)**
> . . . some are exciting . . .

CUT TO:

3. EXT BOWLING GREEN   DAY

CLOSE UP – RUMP OF MAN AS HE BOWLS A BALL.

> **MAN (VO CONT)**
> . . . and some are just plain fun.

CLOSE-UP – MAN'S FACE.
SOUND – FARTING NOISE.

> **MAN (TO CAMERA)**
> Uh oh.

CUT TO:

4. INT LAVATORY STALL   DAY

MAN IS SEATED ON TOILET, PANTS ROUND HIS
ANKLES.

> **MAN (CONT, TO CAMERA)**
> But some things just give me the sh . . . (BLEEP).

HE HOLDS UP A PACKET OF 'YOUNGMAN
INCONTINENCE PADS'.

> **MAN (CONT)**
> So if you're getting on in years and don't want the
> sh . . . (BLEEP), try Youngman Incontinence Pads.

HE TAKES ONE OUT OF THE PACKET AND RUBS IT
AGAINST HIS FACE.

MAN (CONT)
Hmm. Soft as a cloud, strong as an ox,
absorbent as a million sponges.

CUT TO:

5. INT ULTRA-LUXURIOUS TOILET SET   <u>DAY</u>

AS MAN EXITS THE STALL, A DOZEN CHORUS
GIRLS AND BOYS IN GLAMOROUS SEXY COSTUMES,
DANCE ROUND HIM SINGING TO THE TUNE
OF 'YMCA'.

CHORUS
(sing) Youngman

Incontinence Pads

MAN
(sings) Get them.

You know you'll be glad

CHORUS
(sing) No more.

Unsightly stains.

MAN
(sings) It's just like

coming in from the rain.

CHORUS AND MAN
Youngman.

CHORUS FREEZE WITH SMILES.

MAN (CONT)
They do a great job on big jobs, too.

HE WINKS.
END.

*

Frank String drifts through *Nosferatu*, entering rooms he'd forgotten about decades ago. Webs and rat droppings abound. His wanderings take him out to the back. Once he had a garden, a pool, a tennis court. Gone. There the olive trees, there the Moreton Bay fig. The kids climbed them. Gone. Now, just a metre from his door, apartment buildings. They block the sun all day, every day.

*

The Young and The Naked was supposed to be Frank String's renaissance. He'd prove his talent all over again and *make* them see. He'd prove – in a woefully produced, woefully acted, hastily and woefully scripted soap opera – that Frank String was an actor.

So he'd worked harder than he ever had to make old man Bellbird a real *person*, with a *past*. A *man*. Sometimes, he thrilled some of the younger actors with the truth of his performance. You could see their eyes form big O's of wonder at the breadth and depth he brought to what might have been just another scene in just another storyline in just another soap. He infected the cast with his love of the craft. Even when he was flirting with them, he'd still be giving them good advice. Listen, he'd tell them. Listen to what the other person's saying, then don't say anything until you absolutely have to. By which he meant that the audience was in love with the human face – anyone's face – and, if you were truly listening and then truly trying to come up with a true reply, then the audience would happily wait forever for the words to come from your mouth.

The directors hated the way power flowed to the old guy, how the teenyboppers and surf studs would listen, awed, to the real thing – acting, finding meaning in trash, squeezing life out of cardboard. The directors hated the way the show seemed to slow down with all these fucking young wankers listening and waiting and truth-telling a la String. They'd hurry the kids up. Keep it moving. Say the lines.

Yet . . .

it worked.

TY&TN got better. Some nights, it was even very good. And word spread through the biz and the punters, that if you tuned in, you could be sure that any scene with String – no matter which wooden 'star' or drunken has-been veteran was sharing the screen – that any scene with String would feel right, would feel true.

*

The Channel 3 contract allowed Frank String to take prestige film roles or even short stage seasons. ('You're family, Frank.') String waited for film and theatre offers. None came. He did interviews. Magazines. Papers. Chat shows.

Nada.

He accepted a contract for Youngman incontinence pads. It would keep the banks at bay for a little while and – who knew? – maybe they would remember his sly knack with song-and-dance and bawdy humour. The advertising company decided to rush the commercial to air. After all, Frank wasn't getting any younger.

❋

As soon as he saw the ad, he knew he'd made a grave mistake.

❋

THE CITY PRESS.
FRANK STRING GETS INTO NAPPIES.
Once he was a Hollywood heart-throb, then he was the country's
premier acting legend, then he came home to play the crusty
but benign Harold Bellbird on TY&TN. Now he's
spruiking the joys of nappies for grownups. In the
words of the immortal Bard, 'How the mighty
have fallen down.' The ad agency . . .'

TV TRUMPET
ITEM: Frank String not only has egg on his face
but poo in his pants. He . . .

❋

Frank heard it. He couldn't bear to look at it anymore.

No more./ Unsightly stains./ It's just like
coming in from the rain./ Youngman./
They do a great job on big jobs, too.

❋

He'd thrown away his career, his life, his everything.
He was a joke.

Nappies.
Grownups.
Great.
Job.

On.
Big.
Jobs.

Frank trudged down the corridor and entered Nosferatu's huge, ancient, original kitchen. It had three gas stoves, all the better to cook and cater for the glittering part-goers from long-gone glory days. The stoves, like the kitchen, were dusty and dirty. Cobwebs and rat droppings.

He readied his head for the oven and himself for eternity. He turned on the gas. No sound. No smell. Frank remembered they'd turned off the gas last year for non-payment.

'Shit.'

Tears of self-pity welled up and he sobbed and cursed.

'Shit! Shit shit shit shit! Fuck!'

He kicked the stove and WHACKED! a shin.

'Ahh!'

He hopped around on one foot. A bubble of laughter burst out from somewhere deep, deep inside him; a bubble delighting in the ridiculousness of it all, in the life's-a-bitch-then-you-die-ness of it. He turned off the non-gas and started upstairs to his room, switching from howls of grief to howls of laughter, not knowing from second to second which howl would be next, which emotion he would feel this time; and then not caring because, as the actress said to the bishop: Tomorrow is another day, Bishop, and if you want to die right, for Christ's sake pay the fucking gas bill.

16.

BREAK AND ENTER

Smokin' Joe was looking good. After his triumph at the Rising Sun, everyone commented on how he'd managed to cut down his opium intake long enough to help around Miss Bliss by cleaning the odd toilet, spa, whatever. He was excellent at making the windows glisten but he tired after an hour or two; then he'd slink out to his beloved back alley, sit on the milk crate, light up and chase the Dragon till it was time to go home.

'See?' said Ma to the doormen. 'Heaven is smiling on my kindness to poor Joe.'

'He keep keepin' da windows dat clean, we get him *another* blowjob.'

Mr Ma and the doormen were proud as could be of their boy.

*

D.C. Lilly and Specialists Constables Webster and Savage were also proud of him. The whole of Miss Bliss was now bugged.

'Down to the last toilet,' marvelled Webster.

'Smokin' Joe's part of the furniture,' said Savage proudly.

'Not too shabby,' said D.C. Lilly. And Savage and Webster,

as communication specialists, knew what she'd actually said: 'Where does anyone get that kind of courage?'

*

The break and enter of Stella's apartment was a work of art – so expertly done that she didn't notice till she'd changed into her bathrobe and was brushing her teeth. She looked in the mirror and saw Doorman #2 leaning against the bathroom door jamb, looking at her.

'Dental health ver' important.'

Stella screamed, exhaling toothpaste but #2's hand was over her mouth before any real noise got out. He lifted her effortlessly into the living room. Doorman #1 came out of the study with Stella's camera and laptop, put them both on a table, looked at them quizzically, then at Stella.

'Hi dere.'

#1 and #2 were using the very thickest-of-the-thickest, hardest hard-core, scare-the-round-eye accents.

'We foun' de photos of a certain boat what had some – what dey call em? – bodily parts on deck.'

'Body parts,' #2 corrected him.

'Yeah. Body parts. Sorr'. Anyway, we found de photos on your laptop. See?'

He showed her the photo on the screen. The deck of 'Doc's Pride'. A tiny glimpse under tarpaulin of cages full of dead men.

Stella's eyes were bright with fear above #2's huge hand.

'Da question is – you got any utter photo? Any utter compu'ers or came'as?'

#1 signalled for #2 to release her mouth.

'No,' she said.

'So,' said #1, 'you no got any utter photo or compu'ers or came'as?'

'No other photos. And only one computer, one camera. Only them. I swear. Oh God, I swear. Only them. Take them.'

'Well, tank you, Miss, but we gon' take em anyway. Know wha' I mean? We gon' take whatever we want. Know wha' I mean?'

He took out the camera's digital card, put it in his pocket, dropped the camera, smashed it with a heavy boot.

'Oop. De came'a broke. Dat pity. But I'll take de laptop. Ho-kay wit' you?'

'OK.'

#1's face took on a pained expression as though he hated to be so rude as to ask again. 'You *sure* you haven't got any utter compu'ers or came'as?'

'I swear.'

'It jus', I dunno, it seem like you lyin' to me.' He turned to #2. 'What you tink? She lyin' to us?'

'Could be, brudder.'

He moved to Stella and leant into her face.

He had garlic prawns for dinner.

'You send dese photos to anyone else?'

'No. No. No one.'

#1 looked long and hard into her face. He carefully untied the cord on the bathrobe and slipped it over her shoulders. She was nude to his stony eyes.

'Hey. No bad for an old white chick.'

He reached forward with one languid hand and started to twist her left nipple. And twist it and twist it again. Stella screamed in pain behind the hand. #1 stopped twisting. 'Ho-kay. You *sure* you haven't got any utter compu'ers or came'as?'

113

'No.' It was an answer and a plea.

#1 twisted her right nipple. 'You send dese photos to anyone else?'

'No. I told you. No.'

He twisted both nipples as #2 tightened his grip on her mouth, stifling the scream. #1 looked into her face again, then nodded. #2 released his grip. Stella's knees gave way. She fell awkwardly, comically, bottom-first onto the carpet, looked up at the two giants.

'Tell me all dat again, lady,' said #1.

'There are no copies. None. Only the ones in the computer and the ones in the camera and I didn't send them to anyone.'

#1 looked at #2. 'What ya tink? She tellin' de trut'?'

'Yeah,' said #2.

'Yeah,' echoed #1. He smiled down at Stella. 'Please, Miss, cover up. You emba'ass us.'

Stella pulled her robe around her. The pain in her nipples was awful. The fear was worse. 'Ho-kay, lady. Me and my friend here – we find out you lyin' – we find out you bin to p'lice – we come back. We do dis again. Den we fuck you. Den we kill you.'

#1 crooked a finger at #2 who picked up the laptop. They left without another word. Stella's legs weren't working. She crawled to the door on her knees and deadlocked it, weeping with relief and fear and humiliation.

She rang Ng. He wasn't at Best Rest. He wasn't at One Police Towers. She cried more, then rang Cross.

*

No one knew much about Wild Bill – even his last name. The consensus was he was once a great surgeon in London; or he helped found Doctors Without Borders; or he did nada in Nada; or he was a nada in Nada; and he had a nervous breakdown. The breakdown part seemed plausible since Wild Bill seemed to think he was the reincarnation of a real-life 1870s medico called 'Wild' Bill Harding – the stereotypical drunken doctor in Tombstone. He lived three units down the corridor from Stella and seemed to have no other clothes except a ratty old bathrobe or two.

Cross knocked on Bill's door. It opened wide. Wild Bill was dressed in the trademark dressing gown; he was tall, storky, cadaverous, his hair a shock of long, untidy grey surrounding a bald pate; he was unshaven and incurious.

'I know you, friend. You're one of the sheriff's men.' He squizzed closer. 'What is it, Deputy? Miz Pentangeli? She need seeing to?'

'Well, yeah, Wild Bill. She does.'

*

Wild Bill, doctor's bag in hand, went straight to Stella's bedroom.

'You stay outside, Deputy. This here's female stuff.' He closed the door.

PART 2
INNOCENT MURDER

*'The wicked . . . sitteth in the lurking places
of the villages: and in the secret places
doth he murder the innocent.'*

Psalm 10:8

17.

PRESSURE

The Fuk Chin brothel at 198 South Rd Honeyville was an almost exact replica of the one at Merry St Wuthering Hills from which the anal whore Bam – the customers had called her Bum – had foolishly tried to escape and paid for her foolishness with her dishonourable life. From the outside, Honeyville looked like a normal house. Inside it had eight small cubicles, one true bathroom and a portaloo. The garage slept a dozen girls – all Asian, all illegal immigrants. Like Merry St, it had barred windows and razor wire three metres high all round the back fence.

Six girls escaped this time. *Six.*

Ma learnt the facts from shame-faced doormen. It was a slow night for a Friday. One of the girls had stolen a copy of the front door keys a month before. The girls waited. Around 11, the front doorman, bored, got drunk, fell asleep. Six girls just walked out the door. Five were captured easily. The sixth – pursued, like Bam, by a Fuk Chin car – threw herself off the old railway bridge in Station St. The fall didn't kill her. A minute later, the 10.48 outbound from the city did.

Specialists (MVC&IP) were called in. They determined

the dead woman, the client, was Laotian. Visitor's visa up-to-date. No close family members here or there. No suspicious circumstances. The state payed for a cheap cremation.

*

Word came down that night from a high-ranking politico to Doc Mortaferi who passed it on to an associate of Ma. The present state of affairs was not satisfactory. Ma was letting down the side. The Premier claimed that there were no sex-slave rings. How was it possible that sex slaves kept escaping and ending up dead?

'Tell Mr Ma, with all respect,' said Mortaferi to Ma's associate, 'that if he can't fix it, I will.'

*

Ma got the message. Alert but not alarmed, he held a meeting with Doc in Saint Nicholas of Myra's church, North Sweethurst. Doc prayed in one pew, Ma prayed in the one behind. A doorman and one of Doc's crew kept guard while suffering Jesus looked down.

'No disrespect, my old friend,' said Doc softly.

'None taken,' said Ma softly.

Both knew they were both lying.

'I know how to fix this runaway problem,' said Ma.

'Our friends will be pleased. How?'

'How else? Death. I will need the boatshed.'

'It's yours,' said Doc.

'I will, of course, pay your fee,' said Ma but Doc waved this away. Money was a trifling thing between old friends.

Ma leant in to Doc. 'I must kill him myself.'

'Not a problem.'

'You misunderstand me, I think. I must kill him myself in the boatshed.'

This *was* a problem. Doc had an iron rule: If you deliver the client alive, my crew kills him. If you don't like that, deliver him dead. If you don't like *that*, go elsewhere.

'Sorry, Ma. Can't do.'

'Please, Doc.'

'I must protect the integrity of the process.'

'I have to kill him myself,' said Ma. 'It's a matter of face.'

'Fine. But not in my shed.'

Ma looked irritated.

'I respect you, Ma,' said Doc, treading carefully. 'You know that. But it's not possible.'

'This man betrayed me.'

'Ma, please. We know how to do these things so they go perfectly.'

'Even so.'

Doc looked back at Ma.

'Doc,' said Ma. 'I'm asking you a favour.'

Ah.

Doc knew what that meant. He had survived for many years because he knew not only who to break but when to bend.

'When?'

Ma glanced at his gold watch. 'Today. This morning.'

Of course, thought Doc. Today. Murder was always urgent and it would always be today.

'OK, Ma,' said Doc. As soon as he said it, he knew he'd made a mistake. 'But just this once.'

'Absolutely. Thank you, Doc. I owe you. I mean it.'

Ma had better mean it. He owed Doc. Big time. They shook hands. Doc's seaside slaughterhouse was all Ma's.

18.

TERRY DEAR

Terry Dear – the silent half of *The Pentangeli Papers* – lived with his parents; that is to say, every now and again he emerged from the cyberworld where he and his computers lived, to eat and drink and shower and void. Only very seldom would he brave the dangers of the real world and the city's notoriously bad bus system and leave the house. His mother, knowing what she did about this real world, would marvel at his courage.

Yet Terry came all the way into Sweethurst to look in on Stella.

*

'Terry, why is it that whenever you leave your Batcave, you dress like an insane man?'

It was true. Terry, even for a gay geek, had rotten clothes sense. Dots with stripes, misbuttoned shirts, mismatched socks and a new weird colour for his hair every week. This week, electric blue.

'Don't start, Stells. I'm here on a mission of mercy to see if you're alright.'

'I'm touched and I'm fine.'

'Yeah. Sure you're fine. You get burgled and slapped around by thugs. They break your camera and *then* take your laptop.'

That, Stella thought, *is the big crime in Terry's mind. How could anyone steal someone's computer?*

Terry looked embarrassed but gathered his courage. 'So, anyway, Stells, how are the, erm, the, erm, body parts?'

'They're called nipples, Terry. I believe men have them too.'

'No need to be vulgar.'

'So *tout le Sweethurst* knows, huh?'

'No. No.' Terry's face was fierce with denial and outrage at the very thought and Stella loved him for his lie.

Of course they know. Which of her enemies wouldn't be rolling phrases around their tongues like 'Always knew she'd get her tits caught in a wringer' and 'Tough titties'? If it were an enemy of mine, shit, I'd be doing it myself.

'Look, Stells, don't worry about *TPP.* I'll look after everything.'

Stella placed her hand on Terry's. 'You've been keeping *TPP* afloat since I started all this detective stuff.'

'Tell me about it. Anyway, it's going great. Showbiz and crimebiz – good combo.'

'Wait till they read about my nipples.'

'Stella.'

'You know how much I love you, don't you, Terry?' Out of the blue. Just like that.

'That's what I hate about real life,' said Terry. 'Once you get away from cyberspace, people start all this love and hate bullshit.'

Stella pushed. 'Terry? Do you love me?'

They locked eyes. Finally he said, 'Yes.'

Pushy Stella: 'Why?'

Reluctant Terry: 'Why what?'

'Why do you love me?'

'Because. Fuck you, Stells. Because you and *TPP* are the best things that ever came into my life, OK? Cos if you were a man ... oh boy. OK?'

'OK.'

Soon she slept. Terry went home glad.

19.

BY THE PRICKING OF

MY THUMBS

Ng could smell it.

It was in the air over Vice Valley, like a gas. Fetid. It rose from beneath the alley, from the sewers and dark places near Miss Bliss and spread. The anticipation of something wicked.

A dreadful deed was being brewed in someone's dreadful mind, so foul, so elemental it had communicated itself to anything with ears to hear and eyes to see, mortal or not.

The semi-wild Valley cats sensed it. They yowled and hissed. They spat out fear. They scratched and fought, trying to discover if any of their race had nurtured the evil thing.

A rat appeared on the main drag. Huge. Big as the biggest cat and so agitated, it was icy calm. It roamed slowly down the exact centre of the drag. Of the few cars still prowling, some drove close by without seeing it. Headlights lit up its yellow eyes, but it kept walking. Some saw it and blamed the liquor and the drugs.

A drunk driver spotted it. He swerved. He drove down the centre. He'd squash it. Mash it up. Road kill. Fuck you, rat. But he missed it. Four tyres, no hits. The drunk's car hit a tree 50 metres down the drag.

The rat didn't even notice.

A dog caught the rat's scent. He ran out of a side street.

I gotcha.

The rat kept walking.

The dog got cagey.

I'll take it from behind. One quick strike.

The rat stopped, turned and waited.

What? What do you want?

It waited, then headed for the dog.

What do you want?

The dog whimpered and backed down. The rat kept coming at him.

What do you want?

The dog howled. The rat kept backing him down, then rushed him, screeching, perfect white rat teeth ready to rip. The dog ran away.

The rat turned and started walking again down the exact centre of the drag.

*

At the back of Miss Bliss, Foo, Fa and Fun got into Mr Ma's limousine. It sped away.

*

Smokin' Joe just missed seeing the limo. It was already out of sight when he turned a corner and stumbled towards Miss Bliss's back alley.

He saw the rat. He sniffed the air. It groaned with fear. It mocked. It stank and warned.

Smokin' Joe could smell it.

20.

THE BOATSHED

Earlier, high pink dawn clouds in the east were peeking through Vice Valley's glum buildings.

The doormen knock softly on the first door of Miss Bliss's sleeping quarters.

Inside, Fun, Fa, Foo and three other girls share triple bunks, sleeping the sleep of the young. The doormen step inside.

'Foo,' says #1.

Foo looks up sleepily. 'What is it?'

#1 speaks basic Thai. 'Guess it.'

Foo shakes her head as irritably as her position allows. 'I don't know.'

'You going home, Foo.'

At first it doesn't register. 'Home?'

'Chang Mai,' says #1, his face wreathed in smiles. 'Mr Ma say you finished contract and show great honour to Fuk Chin and your family and also you.'

Foo looks at the two men.

#2 says in English, 'What's the matter, Foo? You want to work in Miss Bliss all your life?'

Fa and Fun stir as Foo says, 'What about Fa, Fun? What happen to them?'

#1 and #2 smile fit to burst. 'Them too,' says #2.

'Mr Ma is great man,' says #1. 'He know you love each other. Not want separate. Mr Ma have arranged everything. Plus also big bonus. All you.'

It hits them. Foo, Fa and Fun hug each other, leaping in the air with joy. The other room-mates join in. They squeal and holler and wahoo and praise the wisdom and generosity of the great Mr Ma. Foo hugs her tiny bedside Buddha and whispers a prayer. 'Thank you, Lord Buddha.'

'God bress Mis'r Ma,' says a room-mate, a Korean.

'Yeah,' says #1.

'Absolutely,' says #2.

*

The limo is purring. #1 is behind the wheel. #2 opens the back door and bows low.

'In you get, my royal princesses.'

The girls giggle and start to hop in. Mr Ma is in the back. The girls freeze, uncertain.

'Come on, girls,' says Ma, his generous smile wide. 'Hurry. The last one in doesn't go home.' He goes 'Hahahaha' to show he's joking.

The girls get in. They sit on leather, opposite Mr Ma. #2 closes the door, gets in the front next to #1. #1 presses a button. All doors lock. The limo pulls out.

Ma pats one of the girls' knees. 'You look lovely, ladies,' he says. 'Even though I'm an old, old man, I think you three could make me strong as a bull.'

The girls giggle.

'I could bed all three of you all night and all day.' He winks and goes 'Grrrr' to show he means it.

The girls giggle again. Ma strokes one of their faces.

'Lovely. So lovely.'

His hand is soft like the hand of a prince.

'You're going on a boat. I wish I could come with you.'

*

The limo is already out of sight when Smokin' Joe turns the corner.

*

The limo enters Mortaferi's main gate and Foo spots the big boat, 'Doc's Pride'. Ma says, 'See that boat? That will take you home.'

The girls' mouths drop open. Such luxury.

'For us, sir?' says one.

'Yes, ladies.'

'Oh,' they say.

*

#2 opens the limo door. Ma gets out first. He helps the girls out. They cling to his big arms. They wish they could show their gratitude to him more. #1 is right behind. He carries a big brown bag. Ma ushers them to the boatshed. #2 opens the door.

'This way,' says Ma cheerfully.

The lights are already on. Pulleys. Parts. In the corner a huge glass-doored steel and enamel shower. Circular. Recessed. It smells clean and glistens.

#2 closes the door. #1 starts setting up a small video camera and turning on extra lights. The girls look puzzled.

'Happy pictures to show your family,' says Ma.

The girls nod to each other. Mr Ma. Such generosity.

'OK girls. Line up, please.'

They stand in line. Ma's face becomes exaggerated mock ponder. 'Now how am I going to choose?'

Choose?

'Which one is Fun?'

Fun raises a shy hand.

'Foo? Who's Foo?'

Foo raises her hand.

Ma looks at the third girl. 'So you're Fa.'

'Yes, sir.'

Ma looks at #1 and #2. 'What do you think, boys? Eenie meenie minie mo? Or maybe Fa, Foo, Fun; who's gonna be the one. Or both?'

'Both,' says #2 in a strangled voice.

'OK,' says Ma. 'Both.'

'Ready, boss,' says #1.

Ma points a manicured finger at Fa and makes it dance from one girl to another as,

Eenie meenie minie mo.
Catch a young girl by the toe.
If she hollers, let her go.
Eenie meenie minie mo.
Fa, Foo, Fun. Who's gonna be the one?
Foo, Fun, Fa. Maybe you are.
Fun, Fa, Foo. Looks like it's you.

His finger stops at Fun.

*

It is finished.

Ma turns off the camera.

Foo and Fa are behind the glass, centre stage in the shower, handcuffed round a pole. Both have urinated and defecated with terror. Blood splatters, too. #1 and #2 are stripped down to just jockstraps and George W. Bush masks. They are covered in blood and bits of body. Bush #1 has an erection.

Fun has been chopped up so thoroughly with a machete that parts of her are liquid. Over there a finger, over there a toe. Eenie, meenie, minie, mo.

It's a shame, thinks Ma. Too many escape attempts. Too much back-talk. Too much pressure from above. This will show them all my strength. This will show the girls that I own them. This is what happens when you misbehave.

'Wash them. Then yourselves,' says Ma. #1 and #2 turn on the showers and start to strip Foo and Fa. There are fresh clothes in the big brown bag.

＊

Ma walks outside, glad to breath salty air. How sad to have to do these awful things but honour must be guarded vigilantly and ruthlessly. Without honour, the world descends into anarchy and we – all of us – turn into beasts.

Yes.

By nightfall, the boatshed will be cleansed and de-forensiced to perfection. Doc's men will need just one rubbish bag, if that. Fun was a tiny thing.

＊

Ma's limo leaves the mansion. Two men, in a nondescript old car, enter the gates and drive to the boatshed where they will get to work bagging the bits.

21.

STRESS LEAVE

Constable Savage had worked all night from his den at home.

Since the start of Operation Lincoln, he and Webster had taken turns cataloguing the backlog of unlistened-to tapes. Most was rubbish – snores, nightmares, crap chat in the wee hours. He'd flagged the name 'Pentangeli'

Now he got lucky.

OP LINC. 22.2. TRANSCRIPT. MISS BLISS CORRIDOR.
Doorman 1: So you speak to Mr Ma?
Doorman 2: Yeah.
Doorman 1: You tell him she squealed like a pig?
(inaudible)
Doorman 2: He think Pentangeli telling the truth?
Doorman 1: Oh yeah.
(4 second silence)
Doorman 1: I think we should kill her.
Doorman 2: Mr Ma says no.
Doorman 1: She know about the Russian bodies on the boat.
Doorman 2: She got no proof.

Doorman 1: Lets kill her. Even less proof, yeah?
(3 second silence)
Doorman 2: You right.
Doorman 1: Mr Ma, he thank us.
Doorman 2: You right.
ENDS.

*

Savage's forehead was icy but there was sweat there anyway.

'She squealed like a pig.'
'Let's kill her.'
'Mr Ma, he thank us.'
'You right.'

The tape was nearly a day old.

*

Savage rang D.C. Lilly from a public phone. She was in the hippie van with Constable Webster.

Webster answered. 'Yes?'

'Vic. It's me. The boss there?'

Lilly took the phone. 'Yes?'

'They said they're going to kill Stella Pentangeli.'

'Constable. Are you on a landline?'

'Yes boss.'

'Who's going to kill Pentangeli?'

'I just transcribed flagged tapes. Ma's two main apes were speaking yesterday. They sounded serious.'

'Have you informed Investigator Ng?'

'No, boss.'

'I'll handle that.'

She hung up. She signalled Ng and spoke into the mic.

'Ng. Meet me in the van. Come in.'

'Is it a priority? Come in.'

'Yes. Come in.'

'Out.'

'Out.'

Joe struggled to his feet and weaved his way down the alley past doorman #3. 'Hey Joe. Where ya goin'?'

Joe mumbled something in Cantonese but the doorman knew Joe's story. He wasn't talking to him – he was talking to his dead wife back in Linlin or Poohbear or some dump back home. Joe argued with her all the way down the street. He rounded the corner and looked back. Clear. He opened the door and was inside the hippie van.

✳

'Investigator.'

'What is it, Deputy Commander?'

Lilly turned to Webster and said, 'Drive to her place. Fast.' Webster slid behind the wheel, started up and drove off as –

'Her? Stella?' He paled. 'Is she dead?'

'No, no. We think she's OK.'

'Think?'

They all felt a chill enter the speeding van and a silence steal over Ng. Webster drove fast and well. The van looked like a pile of rust but the engine was powerful and beautifully tuned.

✳

At Stella's Cross peeked through the spy hole.

'Investigator,' said Cross.

'Sgt,' said Ng.

Cross loosed the chain, sprung the lock, opened the door. A plainclothes police towered on either side of Ng, each with a gun – pointed carefully at the floor – in his hand. Cross thought he vaguely recognised them from Specialists Communications.

'Do we need guns, Sgt?'

'No, sir.'

'We'll go help the boss,' said Savage. He and Webster headed for the stairs.

'Where is she?'

Cross nodded towards her bedroom. Ng brushed past the big man.

*

The curtains were half-drawn, all the better to hide Stella's eyes which were rimmed with red.

'Hello, Ng. Long time no see.'

He sort of hugged her. She sort of hugged back. As always, they were both awkward.

'What happened, Stella?'

She pointed at his Fu Manchu. 'Christ, Ng. That's horrible.'

'What happened?'

Stella looked him over. 'In fact, Ng – no offence – you look like shit.'

He waited.

Finally, 'Two men broke in; gave me a hard time. My breasts.'

'Who?'

'I don't know. Two Chinese men. Big. Dark suits. It had to do with the pictures of Mortaferi's boat.'

'Stella. I am so sorry.'

She remembered. 'Oh.' She reached under the second pillow and took out a photo – black and white, 10 x 8.

'Here.'

Ng glanced at it.

Eight cages.

In the foreground of one cage, a half-face with one eye open, looking puzzled.

A hand.

A half-foot.

A foot.

Eight cages of extra-meaty, double-crunchy shark food.

A sign on the boat's side: 'OC'S PRI'.

'I printed one out. I told them I didn't but I did.'

Then, 'Those fuckers laughed at me, Ng. They humiliated me; then the fuckers fucking laughed at me.'

Ng felt the guilt burrow and spread inside him till it was all he was.

*

Ng exited the bedroom, closed the door. Cross was at the window. Ng moved to him.

'She's sleeping.'

Cross nodded. 'It's weird. She goes out like a light. You never know if it's gonna be two minutes or two hours. Then, pow! she's back. Wild Bill says she'll be OK.'

Ng nodded. Cross touched his arm. *It's like stone. Like he's ready for war.*

'Investigator?'

No response.

'Investigator? I got something I better tell you.'

Ng came back from wherever he'd been. 'Yes, Sgt?'

'I think maybe I know how Ma's boys found out she had photos.' Cross looks embarrassed. 'I think I was bragging about it at The Cops Bar.'

Long silence. 'I see,' said Ng.

'I was drunk,' said Cross. 'I was stupid.'

'Do you have a gun?' said Ng.

'Officially, no.'

'And unofficially?'

Cross opened his jacket. 'Beretta 9000. Ten shot.'

'Do you have spare ammunition?'

'Plenty.'

'Good. Guard her.'

*

Unit 9, Chatsbury Mansions. Wild Bill opened his door.

'Ah, Sheriff. Thought it might be you.'

'Hello, Bill. May I come in?' said Ng.

'Sure. Take a load off.'

Bill's unit was the size of three Famous Guest House rooms and not much fancier. Utilitarian. One table, four chairs, camp cot, Salvation Army odds and ends; nothing that couldn't be replaced for under 50 dollars. The only luxuries were the scores of magazines, comics and books, all concerned with the American frontier, post-Civil War.

'I know what you're thinkin' – monomania, right?'

Ng, surprised, smiled and shook his head. 'No.'

'Sure you are. But mainly you're thinkin' ... how is she?'

'Yes.'

'Bruised but ain't nothin' permanent. I don't think them boys were tryin' to do nothin' but skeer her.' He looked at Ng shrewdly. 'You look like you could use a drink.'

'I don't drink.'

'What? *Never?*'

'No.'

'Hmm. Sit.'

'No thank you. I ...'

'Sit.'

137

Ng sat. Bill sat.

'So, Sheriff, what's this about?'

Ng tried to select the right words but was finding it difficult. Ng isn't a tactile man, thought Bill. Touch, emotions, contact discomfit him.

'I allowed her to get involved with dangerous men,' said Ng.

Like Ng, Bill had spent a large part of his life waiting for the next sentence. The important one. He waited. Finally, Ng: 'They know where she lives. They can come back any time. They *will* come back.'

'So? You're the sheriff. Arrest em.'

'They're protected.'

Bill's grizzled eyebrows went up. 'You mean – you arrest em and next thing they're back on the street and still after Miz Pentangeli but meaner?'

'Yes.'

'Then it's simple, son. You gotta kill em,' said Wild Bill.

Ng looked into Bill's eyes a long time. He said, 'Don't be silly.'

But Bill knew Ng was really saying, 'You're right.'

Damn, thought Bill. What a team we'd have made in Tombstone.

*

Ng and D.C. Lilly walked round Judas Park, a long way from Vice Valley, Ma and Smokin' Joe. As usual, the park was tranquil – green and brown and welcoming.

'I need to take two days off, Deputy Commander,' said Ng.

'Why?'

'Personal time. Stress leave.'

'No.'

Ng looked at her.

'I know what you're thinking, Ng. Don't do it.'

'I'll need two days.'

'No.'

Silence.

'*Talk* to me.'

'There's nothing I can say that won't implicate you in this thing.'

'What thing?'

He didn't hear. 'Forty-eight hours. I'm afraid I won't be able to be contacted. Camping. Tent. In the outback.'

'Don't do this, Ng. Please.'

Ng walked away.

D.C. Lilly watched him go.

*

Stella toyed lazily with the idea that Ng's visit had been a dream. Dream Ng had come into her room, then WHOOSH! like the superhero she sometimes secretly thought he was, he disappeared. Then her thoughts soured.

Why does he always disappear? What do you do with a man who's married to murder?

Cross moved into 6A Chatsbury to nurse and guard her.

'Does this building have a back entrance?' said Cross. 'Fire escape or something?'

Stella had to think about it. 'There's an old backstairs nobody uses. It's sort of blocked. Some tenants use it for storage space. Why?'

'Because I'm gonna padlock it. I wanna make sure the only way for anybody to get in is by the front door.'

Stella nodded, then had him take the bathrobe the Chinese had touched and dispose of it.

'That vacant lot off Sweethurst Lane. You want me to maybe burn it there?'

Stella nodded.

Perfect.

*

The Evidence Room at One Police Towers actually covers
two whole floors in the basements, below the holding cells. It
is undermanned by a small group of old, bribable uniforms
who patrol the cages and 'secure' rooms. Drugs are the first
to disappear, then jewellery then porno. Guns, being more
traceable, are the last to go.

Ng directed the Yellow Cab down the ramp, told the driver
to wait, then walked over to the old security uniform. There
were only traces of the addled opium addict left. The Fu
Manchu hinted at Joe but Ng wore one of his impeccably
cut dark suits; a snap brim hat covering his scraggled head;
his movements were elegant again.

'Hello Robert.'

'Investigator. So when are you gonna learn to drive?'

Ng grinned his sad grin. 'Driving and mobile phones
will kill you, Robert,' he said. It was an old joke.

'That goatee's a big mistake.'

'You're right. It's coming off soon.'

Robert opened up the gate. 'So, Mr Ng, what can we do
you for?'

'The Russian men who were killed a few days back, did
we find any weapons at the scene?'

The uniform beckoned Ng with a gnarled finger. 'Step
this way.'

He led Ng past several cages and stopped in front of a
large one, stuffed with boxes, four of them marked *RUSSIANS
(20-3-102-U)*. 'We found enough to start a major war. You
wanna sign any out?'

'I must check for details for the 501s.' The uniform

nodded. Paperwork. He unlocked the gate. Ng entered, took out a pen and pad and pretended to write.

'I better get back, Investigator,' said the uniform. 'Will you lock up?'

'Certainly.'

Robert clinked away. Ng put on gloves and sorted through the boxes till he found what he wanted – a Russian TT self-loading handgun. Perfect. He slipped it into his inside jacket pocket and started to lock up for Robert.

22.

DO THE RIGHT THING

Deputy Commander Lilly slept fitfully these days. She never really needed more than four, five hours but when she worked she'd get less. Cases would invade her head and lodge there. Teasing.

At the beginning, Connie and Minnie had offered her a guest suite at One Police Towers but she'd laughed in their faces. 'You got to be kidding. Police Towers is wired from the basement up.'

'I resent that insinuation,' Minnie had thundered, jowls aquiver.

'I'm not *insinuating*, Minister. I'm stating. I'll put it in writing if you want.'

Connie didn't even bother denying the charge. Lilly was right. They all knew it. Move on. They put her up at La Grande Étoile, where she changed rooms several times till she was sure she was safe from the State police.

Lilly sat at her Étoile window and watched the sun rise over the city. From this height, at this time, it all looked so innocent. Mr Plod, the local constable, walked his jolly beat. The villains were comical, the kids respectful. Arguments were settled over a cup of tea or a pint at the local. The sun always shone in the daytime and the moon by night; and everyone – even Constable Plod – was asleep in an innocent bed. From up here the city works, she thought. From up here it's lovely.

Except. Her lover was a billion miles away in Canberra. Suddenly she ached. She wanted to ring Tiga, to whisper in her ear how much she loved her, how she missed her. Tiga would be asleep now – and she hated being woken up by telephones. When Adrienne was home, Tiga turned off all phones at night and only Adrienne's mobile was allowed (emergencies, on hummer, under her pillow, no exceptions). Lilly took a long hot shower. She eased her hands down to the secret places Tiga kissed, and came and came but she still ached.

She ordered a Le Big Petit Déjeuner from room service, then asked herself the question she'd been avoiding. Ng's friend – lover? – had been invaded, humiliated, tortured. They planned to come back. Ng wanted them dead.

What would she want, if some goons had tortured Tiga?

Knock. Knock. The waiter rolled in a tray table and unveiled bacon, eggs, sausages, toast, tomatoes, coffee, orange juice. He left. Lilly started to wolf down the meal.

What would she want? No, what would she *do?* She pictured Tiga and all possibilities fell away. Yes, she thought, of course she'd kill them. And she'd do it Ng's way – cover her tracks and fake the paperwork. Manufacture the perfect alibi. Then, like Ng, she would wrap the secret into a tight and airless package, go to a secret place in a secret forest where there was a secret well that reached all the way to the centre of the earth. She would drop the package down the well and never ever speak of it again.

Two murders. Could she live with that?

She chewed on a piece of extra-buttered toast.

Sure she could.

✱

She rang Connie at One Police Towers. For once Lilly seemed unconcerned that the phone might be tapped.

'Commissioner.'

'Deputy Commander. How goes it?'

'Fine. Thank you. I've given Ng, Savage and Webster two days off. They're exhausted. We've closed up shop and start again first thing Monday. Ng's gone camping.'

'Ng? Camping?'

'That's correct. A tent. In the outback.'

'*Ng*? In a tent in the *outback*? (pause) How do we reach him?'

'Sorry. We can't,' said Lilly.

Silence. 'Deputy Commander, how about you tell me the truth?'

Lilly didn't hesitate. 'Ng's gone camping in the outback. In a tent.'

'Where?' said Connie. 'Where in the outback?'

'I'm not sure. Sorry.'

'Bullshit.'

'Nice speaking to you, Commissioner.'

Lilly hung up. Kill them quick, Ng, she prayed. And don't fuck up.

23.

MAMMY CROSS

Elias Zwik rang the doorbell of 6A. Cross opened the door.

'Zwikky,' said Stella. She was on her sofa, in pyjamas and Ugg boots, a blanket wrapped round her.

'Well, don't you look chic.' He looked at Cross, who wasn't budging. 'I thought I'd pop in.' To Cross. 'May I?'

'Let him inside, for God's sake.'

Cross stood aside. Zwik headed towards Stella.

'Make this visit short,' said Cross.

Zwik stopped in mid-stride and turned. 'And who might you be, sunshine?'

'A . . .'

Stella jumped in. 'Elias Zwik. Rodney Cross. Cross. Zwikky. Cross works for – with – me.'

Nod and half-hello from Zwikky. Nothing from Cross. As the wise man said, Sometimes it's better to take an instant dislike to someone and save time.

Zwik turned back to Stella. 'Are you sick?'

'Yeah. No. I . . . had a run-in with some bad guys.'

'*What?*'

'That's why this has gotta be a short visit,' said Cross. (i.e. 'You've offered your commiserations, now piss off.')

'I'm guarding her,' he added.

Cross and Zwik checked each other out and it was like a long cold night. Zwikky read the signs of every emotion fretted across the big man's face. Giant angry signs. Jealous signs. Stay out of our world signs.

Zwikky turned back to Stella. 'I've been missing you,' he said.

'You have?'

He sat on the couch, took her hands in his.

Dry and warm. Stella left them there.

'Yeah. Channel 3's not the same without you running around being Sherlock Holmes.'

'Thank you, Watson.'

'Stella,' said Cross.

Zwikky said, 'Your big friend sounds like Mammy.'

'What?' said Cross.

'I said you sound like Mammy. *Gone With The Wind.* Stella's Scarlett, I'm Rhett. You're Mammy and you disapprove.'

Stella stifled a giggle. Cross did look like Mammy or a giant ten-year-old who'd just caught his mother kissing the milkman.

'If you're up to it, Stella, maybe you'd like to come back to the cabin for a day or two?' said Zwikky, all innocence.

'That's not a good idea,' said Cross.

'Why's that, Rodney?' said Zwikky.

Rodney?

He took a breath, exhaled it. 'I told you. I'm guarding her.'

'Then it'd make sense to take her to a place no one knows about.'

'It'd make sense if you shut the fuck up and keep out of . . .'

'Cross,' said Stella. 'Zwikky's right. He's got a place in Lofty Range. It's the perfect hideout.'

Cross lowered his voice. 'Investigator Ng wants me to look after you.'

Stella, hissing: 'Does he?'

Cross, hissing: '*Yes*. He's *worried* about you.'

'If he's so *worried*, where the hell *is he*? I've seen him *once* in *two* months and he stayed half a *second*.'

'He stayed three hours.'

'Who's counting?'

'*You* are.'

'I'm going to Zwikky's.'

'You are not.'

'Am too.'

'Stella.'

Zwik grinned. 'Now you sound like Stanley Kowalski.'

'Who?'

*

Ten minutes later, Stella and Zwikky left.

*

Cross broke into Stella's VW and hot-wired it. He followed Zwikky's BMW. Even with his hooks, he was smooth as ever.

24.

#1 AND #2

Snatches of laughter drifted across the street. It wasn't yet noon, but Miss Bliss was jolly and boisterous and happening. Doormen #1 and #2 grinned and backslapped favourite customers – two big men who loved their job. Big tippers slipped big tips into their hands. Revellers and regulars stumbled out of the brothel; cabs pulled up and regulars went in; hail-and-farewells were exchanged.

'Try the new girl. She's hot.'

''Lo. 'Lo.'

'T'ank you.'

'Yeah.'

Smokin' Joe hobbled across the street, gibbering in Cantonese, scared, agitated. 'Mr Ma. Mr Ma. Need you. Need you.' He was breathing heavily. He didn't do much running these days.

Doorman #1 led Joe away from the door. 'Joe,' he said, 'calm down.'

Smokin' Joe made himself speak clearly. 'Mr Ma. He want see you. See you. Unnerstan'?'

#2 joined them. 'What's he saying?'

'He saying de boss want to see us.'

Joe thrust a piece of paper at them. 'Note. Mr Ma give me dis. He say give *you*. Give *you*, yes?'

#2 took the note. It was printed in block letters. Terse. Mr Ma always wrote in block letters. Always terse.

WUTHERING HILLS PARK NOW. THE GROVE. BRING THE WOMAN'S COMPUTER. BRING JOE. TELL NO ONE. QUICK. M.

#1 reached for his mobile phone.

'No! No!' screamed Joe. 'Mr Ma say no phone. No phone.'

#1 and #2 exchanged looks.

'Must *hurry*!' screamed Joe.

Joe's terror was so convincing and off-putting that neither man stopped to wonder how it was Smokin' Joe's English had improved so quickly.

#1 rushed inside to grab the Pentangeli woman's computer. #2 got the black limo. Joe sat in back. Within two minutes, they were heading for Wuthering Hills. The traffic was light, the run was clear.

'Why would Mr Ma give a note to Joe?'

'Why dis park? It where we did Bam.'

'Got a bad feelin' 'bout dis.'

'Hey, Mr Ma in some kind of trouble. He send for us. We go. End of story.'

*

They pulled the limo to a stop and looked around carefully. Across the small oval was the grove where they'd buried Bum. It was dark. They could see no one.

#2: 'He said go to de grove.'

#1: 'Could be lotta people dere. Like Russians or p'lice.'

149

They both had the idea at the same time. #2 turned round and smiled at Joe. 'Hey Joe. Wanna do us a favour?'

'Anyt'ing for Mr Ma.'

'Good man.' #2 pointed with his finger. 'See dem trees dere. Go see if Mr Ma dere.'

Would he take a bullet for Mr Ma? Absolutely. Such was Smokin' Joe's love for his friend and protector that he didn't even hesitate. He opened the door and gimped gamely across the oval in size-14 boots – way too big for him.

The doormen watched carefully as Joe entered the grove.

Silence. Then Joe's scream: 'Hurry!'

The doormen unholstered their guns and ran across the oval. Ng was behind a bush just to the side of what had been Bam's resting place for a little while. He wore thin gloves and carried a Russian TT.

'Mr Ma?' said #1.

'Joe? Where are you? Where Mr Ma?' said #2.

PHT. PHT.

Two bullets slammed into the back of Doorman #1's head. Even as #2, puzzled, turned towards the sound –

PHT. PHT.

Two bullets crashed into #2's forehead.

POP!

#1 fired his gun into the ground but it was just death reflex. He was long, long gone. #1 and #2 stood stock still for seconds as though they were actors who'd messed up the scene and knew the director would want another take. Then they fell together onto Bam's grave.

Ng drove the limo away, very careful to be very careful. He knew what a poor driver he was – especially at times of stress.

*

At Best Rest Motel, Mrs Puccini and her idiot son Ned were relieved to see their only permanent client put his key in the lock of Room 11. They hurried to him. He often disappeared for a day or so, but *seven weeks?*

'Where've you been Mr Ng?'

'Official business, Mrs Puccini.'

'You look awful. That beard. Tsk. Ned. Go get some of that ravioli on the stove. And the bread.'

'Yes, Mummy.'

Ned rushed off. She looked sternly at Ng. 'You gonna eat something. Now.'

Ng nodded his head obediently. She followed Ng into Room 11. Small, self-contained, clean, anonymous. Home. Mrs Puccini had been airing the room. Good.

'Sit.'

Ng sat at the small standard motel-ugly table. Ned rushed in with a tray – a steaming bowl of spag bol drowning in parmesan, a long stick of home-made bread, orange juice. He placed them on Ng's table, then mother and son stood back to watch. Ng smelt the aroma and nodded at them.

'It smells delicious.'

'Eat.'

Ng speared and twirled and blew off some heat.

'It's hot,' explained Ng.

Mrs Puccini and Ned waited.

Ng blew on the pasta some more, then took a mouthful.

They waited.

'Wonderful.'

Mrs Puccini nodded, satisfied.

Ned was terrified of most people but, with Ng, he was only shy. 'I made that for you, Mr Ning.'

'I saw you, Ned. You're a good boy.'

Ned nodded, pleased. He and his mother exited Room 11.

Ng locked his door, wolfed down the food, tore at the bread with his teeth and had never tasted anything as delicious. Then he slept.

*

Between his other duties, Ned kept a good close eye on the door of Number 11. He *was* a good boy. Yes. Yes he was.

25.

DIRTY WEEKEND

Zwikky moved to the liquor cabinet. 'Beefeater gin. Double. No ice.'

'Mr Zwik, have you been researching me?'

'Absolutely, Miss Five Angels.'

'You trying to get me drunk?'

'Absolutely.'

He gave her the gin, leant down, kissed her on the lips.

Tobacco. Why's it smell so good on him?

'Why Rhett Butler, Ah hardly know yew.'

'Cornball line,' he said. He kissed her again lightly. 'Ready for my cornball line?' he said softly.

'Sure.'

'OK. I've been wanting to kiss those lips since I saw them.'

'That *is* a cornball line.'

'Thank you.'

'You're welcome.'

Stella leant closer, chest to breast. 'You ready for my next cornball line?'

'Yes, Ma'am.'

'Is that a gun in your pocket or are you just glad to see me?'

'That ain't a gun, Miss. That's a rocket launcher.'

'So you *are* glad to see me.'
'Oh yeah.'
She kissed him.

*

RUSSIAN MOB SLAYS TRIAD MEMBERS!
EXCLUSIVE ON HARD CURRENTLY!

CRIME WARS! TONGS V TSARS!
EXCLUSIVE ON NIGHT, NIGHT!

THE CITY PRESS
GANG MEMBERS SLAIN
'GOOD RIDDANCE' SAYS POLICE COMMISSIONER
The bodies of two F** Chin Triad members were found late today
in a copse in Wuthering Hills Park. Both were shot twice in
the head – the standard Russian Mafia 'hit' signature –
with a Russian-made gun which was found
at the scene of the crime.
The Police Commissioner, in a belligerent statement, said,
'While not condoning murder, it's rather nice to see
these two lads off our streets for good.'

*

God. I'm horny as a high-school girl.

Beneath the boho bum façade, Zwikky was a tender lover – considerate, giving, eager. He lay her on the massive bed and gently kissed her face, then slowly and gently undid her blouse and her bra and kissed his way gently down her neck to her bruised breasts where he was even gentler.

He murmured sorrowfully, 'Oh you poor babies' to each breast as though they were wounded birds.

Oh God!

'Will you please *FUCK ME?*'

'Miss Pentangeli! Language!'

He stood, stripped off his clothes.

Yum. Tan. Muscles. Tiny pot belly.

Lithe body, gym-buffed, brown – except for a central smidge of Speedo white at the groin. He took a pack of condoms from the side table and ripped one open with his teeth – a gung-ho soldier loosing the hand grenade and ready to attack the bunker.

'Get it off, bitch,' he said, half strip-club boss, half parody.

Stella stood, started to remove her clothes.

'Slower.'

She slowed.

'Slower. I want a strip show.'

She was sort of clumsy, sort of not. She stood naked.

'Oh my *God*!'

'What?'

'You're straight out of *Norman Lindsay*.'

'Is that good?'

'Good? It's great. You're *perfect*.'

He moved to her, kissed her gently, lay her down once more. Travel along her shivering belly to the patch. Kiss her first, then lick her, then eat her, then kiss her. Now and again, move up to lap her mouth, then down again to lap inside, then up again, then down till Stella tasted only herself and he stayed down and she came. He looked up at her from way down there.

'That's *one*,' he said and her laughter triggered a second coming.

Oooh yeah.

*

Revel. Flaunt. Take. Give. Enjoy.

Stella liked to watch Zwikky's face light up with lust

when he looked at her. He was a mix of rough trade, sensitive poet, con man and clown. His wit was savage and hilarious and Stella found herself stretching to match him – to beat him – to join him. They sat naked in the sun at the long table out back. They played Scrabble. He won. She won. She'd look down at his penis and just that look would start it moving up and sideways along his thigh and her stomach would turn as though in fright and she'd grow instantly wet. He'd bend her over the table, take her from behind, the table rough on her still-sore breasts, so they'd move inside and he'd be gentle and she'd be tough and demanding.

Gimme. Gimme. Gimme.

He was noisy when he came and she liked that and heard herself joining the wails and he was young and hard and experienced and he was her slut and she was his slut and after they'd talk and laugh and drink Beefeater, he with tonic, she straight and he'd fill his lungs with smoke and blow it out and not care because he was young and hard and he would live forever.

Gimme.

*

Cross camped in Stella's VW behind a clump of trees. The police part of him enjoyed the voyeurism, but a deeper part was appalled at Stella's – what to call it? unfaithfulness? Yeah. Under all that muscle and fat, Cross was a romantic. Ng and Stella were the love story; Cross and Stella were the buddy story. Finito. Zwik and Stella had no place in this universe.

He puzzled over it, but not for long. He was a black and white man and impatient with greys. He decided, I'm here to guard her; to stop bad guys getting her. All the sex stuff is none of my beeswax.

So he drank milk by the carton, ate the local take-away pizza, relieved himself in the bushes. Does the ex-cop shit in the woods?

Absolutely.

At some dreary, dreamy stage of half-sleep, Cross heard on the almost-silent radio, 'Police have found the bodies of two Chinese men believed to be members of a criminal gang. Their bodies were found in Wuthering Hills Park. Both had been shot in the head at point-blank range. Specialists MVC&IP are investigating.'

Hmm, thought Cross. Something interesting has just hit the fan. He'd bet his other hand Ng had something to do with it.

26.

POUR ENCOURAGER
LES AUTRES

Ma ordered all Fuk Chin brothel operators to close by 7 am Sunday morning. The whores were to be transported to an outer-suburban amateur theatre building, The Happy Hill Drama Theatre.

'Tell the women they've been so good, you're taking them on a picnic or something,' Ma told them.

Happy Hill Drama Theatre was perfect. It had a nice-sized parking lot. It would seat two hundred something girls and could be easily secured front and back.

*

8 am. Six cars and six buses rolled up into the parking lot. The girls were happy and giggling, delighted to be out in the air. They'd spot an old workmate or friend from the old country and squeal with excitement and hug and kiss them.

'Quiet!' roared one of the owners. 'We picnic here. The food's inside.'

They said 'oh' and 'goodie' and 'yum yum' and scurried inside, aware that – picnic or no – the owners and pimps would beat them for being slow. Inside, they saw all the lights were on. There was a giant-screen TV on the stage. No food. As the last girl entered, a man in a Carnival Punch mask slammed the door shut.

A second Punch stepped onstage. 'Come down front. Sit. And be quiet.'

Two more men appeared onstage. They wore balaclavas. They jumped off the stage and wandered down the aisles as,

Punch 2: 'You move from your seat, you make a sound, you get hurt.'

The girls went silent.

Punch 2: 'Watch.'

He snapped his fingers. The house lights went off. The video of the massacre began.

Steel and enamel.
Foo and Fa scream.
Two George W. Bushes. They wear jockstraps only.
Chainsaw comes into view. A Bush is holding it.
Other Bush has a machete.
Bush starts chainsaw.

As one, the whores in the theatre scream and most never stop.

Chainsaw slices off Fun's arm below the elbow. She dies or
faints and falls heavily, face puzzled.
Other Bush takes off her head with three machete blows. He
vomits through the mask's eyes and mouth, drops the machete.
Bush takes the machete and attacks Fun's body.
And on.
And on.
Bush eases erection out of jockstrap and ejaculates.
More.
Ends.

*

The house lights went up. Mr Ma strode onstage. He said just this: 'Do your duty.'

He exited. Two girls made a run for it and were beaten by Balaclavas 1 and 2.

Punch 2 spoke. 'Quiet.' The girls were still.

'You go back to your work now. You tell no one what you saw.' He looked around the cowed audience. 'But you remember and you be good. Do your duty like de boss says.'

Some of the girls even nodded, Yes I'll be good, I'll do my duty.

The front doors opened. Punch 1 and Balaclavas 1 and 2 formed a line of honour. The girls stumbled out and back to their owners and went back to work.

27.

THE DEATH OF
SMOKIN' JOE

Another screening at Miss Bliss – the jewel in Ma's prostitution crown – was for the more expensive, less-easily-transported property. The doormen were searching Miss Bliss from top to bottom and herding the girls into the parlour. #3 and #4 stood guard. Miss Bliss was secure.

*

Doorman #5 opened the back-door peephole to see Smokin' Joe standing there. #5 was as wide as he was tall. He lifted weights. He boxed. He practised with garrottes and knives. He wanted to make sure he was ready to destroy the enemy. He kept his rage level so high that the enemy encompassed most of the world.

'Go way Joe. We busy.'

'Fuck you. Fuck your mother. Send me your father to suck my cock,' said Joe in elegant Cantonese.

#5 slammed the peephole shut and swung the door open. His butterfly knife was already in his hand, already slicing downward towards the prick junkie's eyes.

Ng stepped close so he was well inside the arc of the slice.

WHAP!

His knee slammed into #5's groin.

CRACK!

The heel of Ng's palm, fingers bent to maximum effect, crashed #5's nose up and back towards the brain. #5 was about to scream but Ng held a hand over his mouth till the brain caught up with the damage and shut him down. Ng lowered him slowly to the floor and headed upstairs towards the sounds from a loud video.

*

The video finished. Ma entered the room, looked at the girls scornfully and said just this: 'Do your duty.'

He left. The girls were herded out. Some walked quickly. Some walked with that stiff-leg motion people get when they're in shock. All had their heads and eyes cast down.

*

In his office, Ma took the massacre tape in his big manicured hands and tore it apart. He used lighter fluid to burn it in the elegant fireplace, careful to wait till even the casing had melted to gas and goo.

He tried to reach #1 and #2 on their mobiles. No. Strange. Maybe he'd been working them too hard. Maybe he'd told them to take a few days off. He couldn't remember. Who cared?

He opened the window to let out the stink from the fireplace.

*

D.C. Lilly taxied to One Police Towers, got the lift to the 11th floor and picked the lock on Hawkeye's office. Specialists (IT, Communications) had arranged a stolen feed to the office of the task force's hippie van bugs. When Lilly learnt of it, she ignored her first instinct and let them keep the feed. They'd know what she knew about Miss Bliss but they wouldn't know she knew they knew, she thought. Which, believe it or not, made sense.

She tuned into Channel Bliss.

*

Ng was unable to watch the massacre tape. He heard screams, chainsaw, bones liquefying. After the movie, he saw the girls, silent, go to their rooms.

Who will confront Ma? thought Ng. Smokin' Joe? Or me?

'Joe.'

Ma was genuinely happy to see him.

'My luck. My brother. How'd you get in? Doesn't matter. Sit. Sit.'

Ma gestured wildly at a chair across from his desk. Ng remained still.

'Oh my friend, these are bad days we live in – and I don't care if you don't understand me. These are bad days. The innocent get killed. The guilty get rich. Surely the heavens will punish me.'

Joe looked at Ma.

'You don't understand a word I'm saying,' Ma said, then lapsed into Cantonese. 'What do you say, my luck? Will the heavens punish me?'

'They'll destroy you,' said Ng in Cantonese.

Ma looked sharply at Joe, sensed a difference in him, shrugged it off.

'I got plans for you, Joe. I'm gonna get you off the Dragon and you'll be my brother. We'll talk. These men around me – they are fools. You are a fool in one thing only – the opium. No more.'

In Cantonese: 'What do you say? Will you let me care for you? Will you be my brother?'

'I am not your brother, Ma,' said Ng in English.

Ng raised his right hand. A gun, Russian, pointed at Ma's face.

'A gun? Joe?' said Ma, puzzled. 'Joe?' he said again. Understanding flooded his voice. 'You a cop, Joe?'

No answer.

'Some of my boys said you were a police. I said bullshit.'

He laughed a well-what-do-you-know-about-that? Gee, the joke's on me.

'You here to arrest me, Joe?'

'No,' said Ng.

'Ah, it talks. The luck, the friend, the brother, it talks. Go away now Joe, please. I'll forget all this.'

'Sorry, Ma. No.'

'You better go away. Or in a week, maybe a month, I'll hunt you down and kill you. Kill you good. Kill your girl-friend too. I'll find your mother and father and brothers and sisters – anyone you have – and kill them too. I'll find your dog and your cat and gut them.'

'I know.'

'If you *know*,' he said, his voice softer, hissing, choked with anger, 'then get the *fuck* out of my office right *now*.'

Ng lowered the gun so it aimed at Ma's heart.

'You're going to shoot me, Mr Smokin' Joe Policeman? In cold blood?'

He pondered that.

'In cold blood?'

Ma glanced over Ng's shoulder.

'No, little brother, you're not shooting anyone.'

WHACK!

A gun barrel hit Ng at the base of the neck and he swam into a dark sea, lit by brilliant flashes of diamond phosphorus.

28.

EXODUS

Mortaferi's raid on Miss Bliss had been a walkover. Doc didn't attend in person but, as usual, he sent his crew in with state-of-the-art weapons – including state-of-the-art-anti-terrorist weapons.

Two Mercedes – one in front of Bliss, one in back. Fake number plates.

Two small, muffled Semtex explosions – THUH! THUH! – one on the front-door lock, the other on the back-door lock and the balaclava crew were in. Four men in front, two in back.

Doorman #6 was no trouble. He raised his hands at the sight of the men. POP! Dead.

#5 was dead or unconscious. POP! to make sure.

#3 was in bed with his favourite whore, savouring her new-found terror. POP! A balaclava man put his finger to his lips. Shh. The girl nodded.

Funnily, the noisiest hit was #4. He was reading a manga porn comic in his room. He said, 'Wha'?' POP! The first bullet didn't do it. He said, 'Ah,' so the balaclava man twisted his neck and broke his spine. CRACK!

Doc's orders were crystal clear: 'Bring Ma to me. Alive.'

A balaclava man WHACK!-ed Ng on the back of the neck and was about to POP! him.

'Wait. Don't shoot him,' said another balaclava man. He spoke into his sleeve, 'Doc, we got Investigator Ng here. Come in.'

Silence. Then Doc's voice in his ear: 'Let him be.'

Balaclava men cuffed Ma and raced him downstairs to the Mercedes.

*

At One Police Towers, D.C. Lilly sent out a code five: 'Officer down. Miss Bliss. Code five. Repeat. Code five.'

She headed for the lifts.

*

From all over Vice Valley and East Sweethurst, uniforms and undercovers in cars and on foot converged on the brothel, guns drawn. But Doc's crew were long gone. Specialists (Hostage and Tactics) were on their way but this was a code five and no street police would wait for those cowboys when there's a fellow officer inside.

A uniform got a megaphone from his trunk. 'This is the police. All people inside Miss Bliss. Come out now. Hands up. No weapons. Do it now. All people inside Miss Bliss.'

Slowly, the women came out, hands up, crying, scowling in fear, laughing with joy, shocked, stoned, some broken, some fixed and it seemed to the police and the gathering crowd that this was a mini-Exodus. The slaves had crossed the Red Sea and there was no sight of Pharaoh's army.

A plainclothes aimed his gun at one of the girls. 'Face down on the street. Now.'

The girl burst into tears and stood there confused.

The crowd started booing.

A Sgt moved to the plainclothes and – even though he was outranked – made the plainclothes holster his gun. He moved to the girl and hugged her. 'No one hurts any of these girls anymore,' said the Sgt.

Ambulance sirens and Specialist (Hostage and Tactics) sirens wee-are-ed quietly in the distance.

In the crush of cars and people, D.C. Lilly reached the scene running.

The megaphone boomed, 'Last chance. Anyone still in Miss Bliss. Come out now.'

They waited for one minute, then two. A tiny Chinese man – head wound, pale face, greasy hair, hands in air, exited Miss Bliss. A few police recognised Smokin' Joe; no one recognised Investigator Ng.

Lilly held her Federal shield high and walked carefully towards Ng but he collapsed before she quite got there.

'Hospital,' she said. 'Now.'

*

THE CITY PRESS
OPERATION LINCOLN
MASSIVE POLICE BROTHEL RAIDS
The dirty rats who imported innocent young girls to work in their sleazy brothels have been caught in traps loaded with the finest cheese: good old-fashioned police investigation. The Premier said today he had initiated a joint task force when he . . .

OPERATION LINCOLN! SEX SLAVES! GRAPHIC FOOTAGE TONIGHT ON HARD CURRENTLY*!*

OPERATION LINCOLN! TONIGHT ON NIGHT, NIGHT!
MAN'S INHUMANITY TO WOMAN!

*

During raids over the next two weeks, no police were killed and only six injured. Seven Fuk Chin were killed and a score injured. When shots were fired at police in Benny Valley, five Fuk Chin were killed within an hour.

Nineteen brothels were closed down. Forty-four people were charged with a total of a hundred offences. Seventy-seven slaves were found. Police guesstimated that a dozen were unaccounted for. Of the seventy-seven, ten were allowed to stay on humanitarian and other grounds. Neither Foo nor Fa qualified and they were deported.

Of the top Fuk Chin, only Ma managed to escape. The rumour was he'd escaped with a million dollars, or millions, or a billion to Singapore or Beijing or Bangkok.

A later limited-distribution internal police report noted rumours that some of the girls turned on their keepers and assaulted them while police looked on or turned away. This could not be confirmed.

There was also a rumour about the two doormen found shot to death in Wuthering Hills Park. Some said they were killed by local Russians or by a hit man from Moscow or, perhaps, an interstate brothel owner or, some said, by local police.

Many second- and third-generation Fuk Chin, abandoning ancient notions of 'strength in silence' and 'death before dishonour', turned informant. The Honourable Fuk Chin Society – the Tiger of Tigers, the Feared of the Feared, the Many-Headed Snake, may it live ten thousand years – just . . .

rolled over onto its back, purred like a pussycat and was euthanased.

The Premier hailed Operation Lincoln as 'one of the great successes of my administration'.

*

Only a handful of people in policio/politico circles knew Ng was even involved in the fall of the house of Fuk Chin. Webster and Savage noticed that even the few who knew the real name of the junkie, Smokin' Joe, never talked about him and never talked about Ng. Ever.

29.

DOC AND MA

Mortaferi's mansion takes on a grimmer tone in pre-dawn night. The security lights. The oceanic darkness.

Two Mercedes pull up. Mortaferi's crew hustle Ma inside. Alfred, ever the efficient butler, is pleasantly welcoming.

'Mr Ma.'

'Alfred,' says Mr Ma, observing the courtesies.

Doc stands at the massive sea window, but his eyes don't leave the view.

'Doc. What are you doing?' says Ma, more hurt than angry.

Doc, to the goons: 'Stick around.' To Ma: 'Come here.'

Ma swallows the discourtesy, walks over to Doc. 'My friend, is there a problem?'

Doc's face is so full of distaste it seems he won't be able to clear enough of the bile away to speak. Finally Doc speaks. 'Did you kill a girl in my boatshed?'

One of Ma's legs starts to shake just a bit. 'Who told you that?'

'*Did you?*'

Ma knows he knows. 'Yes. But. It was only a whore,' says Ma. 'The sluts, you see, they'd been misbehaving. Escaping. You know this, Doc.'

'Did you make a video of killing her?'

'That's my business, Doc.'

'*Did you make a fucking video of it?*'

'Please, Doc. Yes. I only made it to show to the girls, then I destroyed it. May I sit?'

'No. So the tape you made is destroyed?'

'Yes. Of course. I'm not a fool. I destroyed it. One video. One video only. I burned it. I swear on my mother's eyes.'

Doc waits, then nods to himself as though satisfied. 'OK.' He snaps his finger. 'Alfred. Play the video.'

'Sir.' He points the remote at Doc's mammoth TV screen/ VCR/DVD combo and a videotape begins. It shows the mutilation of Fun.

'This isn't my tape,' says Ma.

'No,' says Doc. 'This is the tape *I* made.'

'You spied on me?' says Ma.

'I always have my cameras on. In case ...' But the bile has returned and lodged in his throat. He coughs it away. 'In case my *friends* decide to *abuse my friendship!* by using *my fucking boatshed!* to massacre *a little girl!* while his crew *come in their pants!*' He shakes his head.

'Please, Doc. May I sit?'

'No.'

Ma is a brave man and a proud one but he feels his legs weakening under the rage lifting from Doc like swamp gas. Ma's legs shake so badly, he slumps into a chair opposite Doc.

'Get him off my *furniture.*'

The goons shove Ma onto the floor – and Ma knows, then, for absolute sure, he's a dead man.

'I don't understand you, Doc. You, I, many of us have people killed. Out in the world. In the shed.'

'Not civilians,' says Doc too softly.

'I'm sorry. I didn't hear you.'

'Not *civilians.*'

'I ... what? ... I don't understand.'

'I don't kill civilians. You and I chose this life. The girl chose nothing.'

Doc looks at the screen. Doorman #1 is ejaculating. 'Turn it off.'

Alfred switches off the video. Doc keeps looking down at Ma on the carpet as though he can't believe the species exists.

'You're going to the boatshed, Ma.'

A puddle starts to grow around Ma's crotch and on the carpet. A stench of fresh shit rises from him.

'Even with my worst enemies, I put a bullet in their head first. But I'm thinking, Ma. I'm thinking my boys should forget the bullet. Like you did. That they should start with your fingers and toes. I'm thinking of making my massacre twice as long and a thousand times harder.'

'Please, Doc.'

'Please what?'

'Give me the bullet first.'

Doc looks at his old colleague, nods briefly, rises. He speaks to Alfred and the boys. 'Give him the bullet. And get his mess cleaned up.'

Doc walks off to the garage and chooses a car. He prefers to be somewhere else, somewhere visible – maybe in his BMW cruising Bayside Bay Drive by dawn's early light – when there's slaughter to be done. So he doesn't hear Ma's final words.

'Thank you, Doc.'

30.

WHODUNIT

A sliver of sun slats through a small part in the curtain. It hits Stella in the eye . . .

. . . *like a big pizza pie. That's amore.*

She turns away, buries her face in Zwikky's neck, is asleep again.

*

Both naked on the back deck. *Heal me, Brother Sun.*

*

Spoons. Her buttocks to his groin. Rear entry. Quick. Warm and wet. An 'Oh. Oh. Ah.' screaming match.

Yummy.

*

Ten minutes. Stella is wide awake. Zwikky is dozing.

'You're a stud, stud.'

'What can I say? I know.'

'What about me?'

'Oh, dunno, Five Angels. You're OK, I guess.'

'Thanks.'

'You're welcome.'

'I should be going, Zwikky.'

'Why?'

'The real world.'

He sighs, throws back the sheet, rolls off the bed.

Mummy, his penis is frowning.

'I'll grab a shower.'

'No. *We'll* grab a shower.' Stella's mobile beeps. 'See you in there.'

Zwikky goes into the bathroom.

Here it comes. The real world.

*

'Hello. Pentangeli.' It was Cross's voice. 'I heard some yelling a while back. You alright?'

'What do you mean, you heard? Where are you?' said Stella.

'In your car.'

'What are you talking about?'

'I'm parked up the hill. I'm keeping an eye on you.'

'What? Since when?'

'Since all weekend.'

She jumped up, ran to the window, saw him 30 metres away. 'Cross!'

He waved to her cheerfully.

She ducked out of sight and clambered into one of Zwikky's shirts as, 'You grubby prick! You've been *spying* on me? Why the *hell* have you been spying on me?'

'Investigator Ng told me to.'

'*I'm* your boss, remember?'

'We're associates, remember?' said Cross, standing on his dignity.

'Not any more.'

'I'm coming in.'

'No!'

She slammed down the cell phone. It rang again, immediately.

'I said no.'

But her line was dead. It wasn't her phone. On the bedside table, Zwikky's cell phone rang. She noticed the number of the incoming caller.

0555-6565.

Mo Sherlock.

Stella pressed the receive button on Zwikky's mobile. Mo's voice: 'Zwikky? Zwik, sweetie. That you?'

'Hi, Mo,' said Stella.

'Who's that?'

'Stella. Stella Pentangeli.'

Silence.

On instinct, Stella said, 'It's alright, Mo. Zwikky told me he's been spying for you.'

'He did?'

'Yes. He thinks Sir Rex is onto him.'

'Shit. Put him on.'

'No.'

Stella disconnected. Cross entered through the back door, rumpled and smelly, as Zwikky entered from the bathroom, brown, gleaming, guilty. Cross couldn't help but look Stella up and down with appreciation; Zwikky's shirt looked a lot better on her. It swelled in different and better places. Her legs. Oh, her legs.

Stella looked from one to the other and didn't know who to hate most – the lover who was a spy or the spy who was a friend. 'Assholes.'

She threw his phone at Zwikky's groin. It bypassed the towel and connected heavily.

'Ahh!'

Pure luck.

Zwikky doubled over. 'What the hell's wrong with you?'

Stella ignored him. She turned to Cross. 'I know who dunnit. I know who the spy is.'

Cross beamed. 'Yeah?' He pointed at Zwikky. 'Him?'

'Him. He sold out his own show and Clap to Mo Sherlock and even planted fake evidence on Frank.'

Cross looked at Zwikky. 'Gosh. I had this funny feeling you'd end up being a two-timing greasy piece of shit.'

Stella crossed the few metres and the light years of treachery that separated them and slapped his face. It was pure luck again that her ring connected with his lip. She moved to the bedroom to change.

'Pentangeli and Associates,' said Cross, proudly. 'We always get our man.'

Zwikky tried to come up with a snappy reply but his mouth didn't work properly because of the blood.

31.

PENTANGELI AND CLAP

Shortly after Stella's return from Lofty Range to 6A Chatsbury Mansions, Wild Bill padded down the corridor in his bathrobe to check on her.

'They look jes' fine, Miz Pentangeli. Any pain?'

'Just in my heart.'

He glanced at her shrewdly but left the comment well alone.

'Well, I better skedaddle.'

'Bill. Thank you.'

Stella kissed his cheek and squeezed his hand. He blushed – all Wild West bravado gone.

'You're welcome, Miz Pentangeli.'

*

Frank came by.

'Are you alright, Frank?'

He flashed his old-time 22-carat Hollywood smile. 'Top of the world.'

Stella regarded him warmly. *That's why I love actors. The worse the adversity, the more you shove out your chest and smile. Tits and teeth. Tits and teeth. Don't let them know it hurts. The show must go on. You're the show. Go on.*

Stella put her hand on his shoulder. 'I found out who the real spy was.'

Frank patted her hand absently. 'Good.'

For all the effect the news had on him, she might have said the weather was clearing. Stella removed her hand and tried again.

'It was Elias Zwik. Zwikky.'

His eyes turned inward. His smile faded. 'The thought of a person betraying another has always disgusted me. A man's word is his bond and all that. I mean, if *we're* not our brother's keeper, who the hell is?'

'This is my fault. Is there anything I can do?'

His voice turned cagey. 'Sure, sure there is. You can talk to Sir Rex.'

*

All Stella said to Clap on the phone was, 'I was wrong. It was Zwik.'

'Get in here. Now.'

Stella didn't know whether the urgency was a good sign or a bad one.

*

Norman ushered her into Sir Rex's office. He was pale. He left the room.

From behind his desk, Sir Rex studied her gloomily. 'You sure it was Zwik?'

Stella placed a phone log on his desk. 'Dates and times of phone calls to Mo Sherlock. My associate . . . found them.'

'How?'

'He bribed a policeman with beer and pizzas.'

Sir Rex blanched and said, 'I didn't hear that,' and waved a frantic, imperial hand at her.

Stella put the log away. 'He can also get you the phone transcripts if you want.'

'No. No. (weary pause) Enough.'

Clap looked down at his thick strong fingers as though he'd never noticed them before. He wiggled them, had each thumb attack the other, made them all lie still.

'Zwik was . . . like a son to me.'

And like all good sons, he killed his father.

Norman opened the door.

'Mr Zwik, sir.'

Zwikky entered. Norman stayed. Stella's heart hit the back of her throat.

Zwikky was as sartorially challenged as ever. A cigarette drooped from Zwikky's Band-Aid lip. He looked past Stella and through her. She wasn't there.

Ah, men. You spy on them, fuck em, uncover their treachery, zap em in the balls and slap em round. Then they go and treat you like dirt.

Clap: 'You're history at my network.'

Zwikky: 'You don't actually believe Stella, do you?'

Clap: 'I've had the cabin closed. Your things are on the lawn. When we're done here, get your personal stuff out of my channel and fuck off. Norman, get a couple of guards to escort the cunt. Mr Zwik's a thief. He's stolen enough.'

Including you, thought Stella.

'Yessir.'

'Don't be stupid, Sir Rex. What I did was nothing. A bit of fun.'

'I want your resignation.'

'We're not playing this game, are we?'

'I want your fucking resignation. Now.'

'Oh no. No, no. Fire me.'

He wants his payout.

Clap opened a drawer and threw some pieces of paper on the desk.

'Read them, Zwikky.'

'What are they?'

'Gambling debts. Horses and casinos. *Your* gambling debts. One hundred and eighty-two thousand and change. I own them.'

'I'm not quitting.'

Clap gazed at Zwik. Dandruff on Clap's shoulder. Shit on his shoe. 'Sure you are. Or else I'm selling the debts to Doc Mortaferi's men. They like immediate payment. Plus interest. In full. Or they get dangerous.'

The old man's done him like a dinner.

Zwikky's face was pale above the brown neck, but he grinned his old grin. To Stella's surprise, it had genuine warmth. 'OK, Sir Rex. I quit.' He offered his hand. Clap ignored it. Just like Zwikky ignored Stella as he sauntered out the office with Norman at his heels.

Farewell, my lovely.

'Well. That's that.' He looked Stella in the eye. 'You're quite a woman, Pentangeli. Why did I fire you?'

'Because you were stupid.'

'Want to come back? Work in the biz again?'

'For you?'

'Yeah.'

'No offence, Sir Rex, but I'd rather drink Drano.'

Clap nodded. He saw the basic fairness in her comment. 'So. What's Frank String want? Money?'

'He wants an apology.'

Clap's face turned red. 'I don't do apologies.'

Stella had warned Frank about this – 'He won't apologise. In Clap's universe, it would be like performing hara-kiri with blunt knives.' As in –

SIR REX WRECKS SHOW.
How Channel 3 got it wrong.

CLAP GROVELS. STRING GLOATS!

THE OLD MAN AND THE C
Spied, lies and dirty deeds in a young and naked world.

*

'He doesn't want a public apology. In private, off the record.'

'Why?' said Clap. 'What good's that do him?'

'You don't get it, Sir Rex. You resurrected him. He loves you.'

There was a great silence as Sir Rex pondered this. 'OK. In private. What else does he want?'

Stella opened her mouth, closed it, opened it again, not sure how to put it. 'Well . . . he wants to . . . die.'

*

SHOWBIZ! SHOWBIZ! SHOWBIZ! ONLINE!
THE PENTANGELI PAPERS ***EXCLUSIVE***!
FRANK STRING RIDES AGAIN
In an unprecedented move, Sir Rex Clap announced today that
Frank String – who left TY&TN last week for what were termed
'creative differences' – will be back for one final scene.
Instead of disappearing without explanation, Frank String's
notorious character, Harold Bellbird, will be given a
soap opera's highest honour – a death scene.
Sir Rex said, 'Harold was a horseman and a man of the land.
He should die in the saddle on his favourite mare
in the middle of his estate.'

TV TRUMPET
Elias Zwik resigned abruptly from Channel 3 today. In his
hey-day the producer/writer/showrunner was known as
the Supreme Lord Of Everything Channel 3 Makes.
Zwik would not comment on . . .

*

Channel 3 Writers had been beefed up with a new *wunderkind*
but Ricci-Trish and the W's were given the honour of writing
Harold Bellbird's Last Ride.

'They want, like, the best soapie death ever,' said Ricci-Trish.
'We're gonna, like, give it to them.'

'It writes itself, really,' said W1.

'Writes itself,' said W2.

32.

THE DEATH OF
HAROLD BELLBIRD

Director Peter Mountjoy, the cameraman and her assistant, the makeup-cum-wardrobe man, the horse-wrangler-cum-stuntman, a mare named Coco, a gelding Called Thunder, Colette Keen (aka Brooke Rivers) and Frank String (aka Harold Bellbird). The tiny cast and crew testimony to the secrecy surrounding the scene – the new and secret climax of EP 300 of *The Young and The Naked*. Sir Rex, Norman and Stella were the only outsiders.

*

Earlier, Clap had insisted that Frank and Stella ride in his limo to the set – a long green plain at the foot of a mountain just 20 minutes from the city. It doubled as the fictional Bellbird Estate in fictional Ramsay Valley.

'It was a misunderstanding, Frank,' Clap said. 'Blaming you for spying, I mean. And . . . er . . . firing you.'

'Water under the bridge, Sir Rex,' said Frank airily.

'Jesus, Frank, it was you who wanted an apology.'

'And it was very gracious of you.'

'Fair enough. (Silence) No. No. Not fair enough. To call into question the reputation of a man like you was unforgivable and I'm ... (long pause, clear throat, cough) ... sorry.'

'Thank you.'

Clap caught Stella's eye. She nodded, *Attaboy*.

'It seems to me, Frank ...'

Frank interrupted sternly. 'Will you just shut up about it?'

Clap bowed his head and nodded. 'Quite right, Frank. I'll shut up.'

The Player King insults the King. The King thanks him. Truly, the times are out of joint.

And Stella wondered again at the strangeness of men.

*

'OK, everybody, listen up.' Mountjoy's South London accent was more pronounced than usual; the only sign that he was intimidated by the great man's presence.

'This scene is simplicity itself. It's a lovely morning and Harold is riding Coco the mare. The grand-daughter, lovely young Brooke Rivers, is riding with him on Thunder. Clip clop, clip clop. They stop and gaze over the opulent beauty that is the glorious fabulous Bellbird Estate with Bellbird Mountain in the distance. Cor blimey, ain't it lover-ly. Then Harold says ...'

Mountjoy pointed to Frank who said, 'Life is hard, Brooke. But, O, it's so good.'

'Excellent,' said Mountjoy. 'Then Harold feels a pain in his chest, grabs his arm. Brooke says ...'

He pointed to Colette. 'Grand-dad!'

'Excellent,' said Mountjoy. 'But without the chewing gum, if you please. Next, Harold slumps forward. Poor little Brooke doesn't know what's going on but the wonderfully intelligent horse, Coco, keeps walking towards Bellbird Mountain as though the critter knows where her beloved old master wants to go. Poor Brooke watches. Harold falls from the horse. That will be done by Jim our dare-devil wrangler/stunt man. Brooke gallops over, jumps off Thunder, takes dear old dead Harold in her arms and sobs piteously, the credits roll and there won't be a dry eye in the house. Got that everyone?'

Cast and crew nodded.

'OK. Makeup, costumes, Jim. I want to start the first shot in fifteen. I repeat fifteen. Go.'

*

The first hour went smoothly. The two fine horses trotted and cantered and hit their marks. Harold and Brooke each got their horse-riding close-ups. Then –

33. EXT BELLBIRD ESTATE   DAY

HAROLD
Life is hard, Brooke. But, O, it's so good. So very, very good.

A SPASM OF PAIN CROSSES HAROLD'S FACE.

HAROLD
(grunt)

HAROLD GRABS HIS ARM. BROOKE REALISES
SOMETHING IS WRONG.

BROOKE
Grand-dad.

(UNSCRIPTED. HAROLD, SMILING, REACHES OUT
AND GENTLY TOUCHES BROOKE'S FACE.)
HAROLD SLUMPS FORWARD IN THE SADDLE.

185

COCO STARTS TO HEAD SLOWLY FOR BELLBIRD
MOUNTAIN.

'And . . . cut!' said Mountjoy. 'Nice ad-lib, Frank.'

Coco kept going. The wrangler whistled and hoy-ed the
normally obedient creature but she kept heading for Bellbird
Mountain.

Frank fell from his horse.

'Silly prick,' muttered Mountjoy. 'Trying to do stunts at
his age.' He turned to Colette. 'OK, Brooke, go to him and
start crying when you see he's dead. Sound! Slate! Action!'

33B. EXT BELLBIRD ESTATE   <u>DAY</u>

BROOKE CRIES OUT IN ALARM, GALLOPS
THUNDER OVER TO HAROLD, LEAPS FROM HER
HORSE, TAKES HIM IN HER ARMS, WEEPS.
ROLL END CREDITS.

The make-believe grand-daughter young girl galloped
over to her make-believe Grand-dad who was make-believe
dead, got off her horse and took the old man in her arms,
crying.

'And cut. End slate. Let's move in for the close-ups. *Now*,
please.'

Only Stella noticed at first that Brooke was still crying
and that Harold was not moving. She rushed forward, passed
the director and crew and stopped a metre away.

'Jesus Christ. He's dead,' said the cameraman.

Colette rocked back and forth, her heart about to burst.

'Dead?' said Clap.

'I think so.'

'Shoot it,' said Stella.

'A dead man?' said the cameraman. 'No way.'

Mountjoy saw Stella was right. He unhooked the camera from the stand and went in close on Colette, then moved round the two of them, catching Frank's dead eyes, the mounting agitation of the horses, the tears and snot and wails of grief bursting out of the young girl. At the end, Mountjoy went huge on Harold's face which wore a tiny hero's smile.

You old ham.

'Cut. Thank you. Oh, and today is Frank's last day,' said Mountjoy.

It's customary to applaud an actor's final scene in a film. Mountjoy put the camera back on the stand. Mountjoy and the crew started clapping. Somehow it didn't feel silly as Stella, then Clap, then Norman joined in.

33.

A DISCUSSION
ABOUT MURDER

Everything was the same at Sweethurst Caff. The coffee was hot, the bacon crisp, the eggs over easy. And Stella was eating alone. The afterglow of the Day of The Russians still warmed Cross, and Mona the owner, knowing that Cross and Stella were associates, treated Stella with a new respect and efficiency.

It's come to this. A fat ex-cop with hooks has made me whole in the eyes of Sweethurst. And I'm still eating alone.

'Hey, boss.' Cross entered, saluted her military style, and sat. 'Cross.'

Several luvvies – male and female – checked the big man out. A young curvy blonde – low-cut tight T-shirt, short shorts – undulated to the table.

'Hi Roddy,' she purred.

'Hey there, Lottie.'

'It's *Lola*.'

'Oh. Right.' Cross was firm. 'Lola, doll, no offence but my associate and I need to talk. Business.'

'Like crime business stuff?'

Cross, tough but modest: 'Yeah. Like that.'

Lola shoved her hand out at Stella who took it wearily. 'I'm Lola. You're Stella Pentangeli, right?'

'Right.'

Lola looked at Stella. The look said, Why sit around drinking *café* with an old lady like you? *I'm* here.

'I'll give you my number, Roddy. *Again.* In case you lost it.'

'Thanks, doll.'

Lola bent over and, fine breasts gaping and obscuring Stella's face, wrote on the napkin. Very. Very. Slowly. Stella was stoic. She guessed that Cross was fixating on the gape.

Oh yeah, Lola, thought Stella. *He'll be calling you real soon.*

'OK. Bye-ee, Roddy. Bye-ee Mrs Pentangeli.'

'Bye-ee.'

Lola shimmied away. A waiter brought Cross his eternal usual – hot chocolate and two hamburgers with the lot.

'Thanks, pal.'

'You're welcome, Rodney. More than.'

Christ. Even the waiters are vamping him.

'I wasn't kidding Cheetah about us needing to talk.'

'Lola.'

'Yeah.'

Stella waited. 'So? Talk.'

Cross looked at her, then round the Caff, then at the floor. Finally –

'Those two Chinese guys who were shot in the park.'

'What about them?'

Cross repeated the cycle again. He looked at her, then round the Caff, then at the floor. 'They were the guys who broke into your place.'

Stella paled. Her mouth went dry. She said nothing.

Cross coughed. 'It seems to me ... it's a ... weird coincidence that the Russians did those two. And ... it was very good shooting.' Cross looked at the menu. It was upside down. 'Anyway, I was wondering if ... if you've spoken to anyone.'

She knew Cross was trying not to say something he was trying to say. 'Spoken to anyone? As in spoken to Ng?'

'Yeah.'

And she knew. And she knew she'd known since she heard about the killings in the park.

Christ, I'm going to faint.

'Boss? You OK?'

No.

'Yes.'

Get it together. Faint later.

'Where is he?'

*

Stella walks from the car park to hospital reception and thinks how many dead, dying and maimed people have passed through her life since Ng. The nurse at the desk recognises her and, even though visiting hours are strictly enforced, waves Stella through. 'Ward Three. Registered as Mr Dun.'

Doctor Butson spots her, tips her a wink. 'Stella. How are the nipples?'

Ah, City Hospital – my second home.

There are six beds in Ng's ward, all occupied. Stella barely registers the other patients – only Ng, pale in a lime-green gown, looking out the window next to his bed.

'Ng,' she says.

He turns, starts his shy and reluctant smile, then stops. 'Stella.'

She sits primly on the chair next to his bed, leans in, and whispers, 'Tell me you didn't kill those men – the Chinese.'

She wants him to lie; to look her in the face and deny it.

Please.

'I'm afraid I did.'

'Kill them?'

'Yes.'

She waits for him to go on – to justify, explain, excuse – to get them both off the hook. He is silent.

'Did you . . . I mean . . . was it self-defence?'

'In a way. But . . . no.'

'It was because they hurt me?'

'Yes.'

He could have added, It was my fault they hurt you.

Or, They would have come again.

Or, They massacred a girl. They used a chainsaw and a machete.

But just 'Yes.'

'I see.'

Suddenly Ng is more tired than he's ever been. 'It was my doing, Stella. Only mine.'

Stella stands. 'Bullshit. I don't know how to live with this.'

The end. Nothing more to say. She turns, half-hoping Ng will come up with a last minute lie – anything.

Nada.

She walks out.

*

It takes an hour or so, then an ache starts in Ng's chest and gets worse. Next to the ache is a hole that gets emptier. Against doctors' advice, Ng checks himself out of hospital.

34.

A DISCUSSION ABOUT
INNOCENT MURDERS

Ng lifted the shiny brass horse shoe on the massive oak door. BANG! echoed through Doc's mansion and Alfred opened the door with the usual promptness. 'Investigator Ng. Good to see you, sir.'

'Get Mortaferi.'

The butler hid a 'tsk, tsk.' He had never gotten used to the tiny policeman's rudeness. Ng – the back of his head bandaged – brushed past carrying a nondescript plastic shopping bag.

'Oh dear. That's a nasty bump. Are you alright?'

'Get Mortaferi.'

'I shall see if Mr . . .'

Doc entered from the depths of his home and, as ever, tried to make nice. 'Mr Ng. What a pleasant surprise.'

Doc didn't bother extending his hand. Ng never took it.

'Alfred. Drinks. What are you having, Mr Ng?'

Ng turned to the butler. 'Get out. Stay out.'

This time Alfred's 'tsk, tsk' was audible.

Doc sighed. 'If you could leave us alone for a tick, Alfred.'

'Does sir still wish a drink?'

'No, no. Thanks, no.'

Alfred exited with dignity.

Doc looked Ng over, amused. 'You look like shit.'

No answer.

Doc moved to the massive glass wall that overlooked Bayside Bay. He tapped the glass with a gold ring. 'Remember when you got some friends to take pot-shots at me through this window?'

No answer.

'Coulda killed me if you'd wanted to. Anyways, I got it bullet-proofed. Cost a fucking arm and a leg. Tell your friends.'

Doc sat down, half facing the calm ocean, gestured for Ng to sit and – surprise – Ng did. A faux-marble coffee table separated them.

'Why didn't you kill me at Miss Bliss?' said Ng.

Doc grinned. 'You must learn to come to the point, Mr Ng. Stop beating about the bush.'

'Why didn't you kill me?'

Doc looked innocent, offended. 'I don't know what you're talking about. What's a Miss Bliss? It sounds like a brothel. Is it?'

Ng shrugged. He reached into his shopping bag, slipped a surgeon's glove on his right hand, took out a micro-cassette, pressed the button.

> MA: *Then, in a week, maybe a month, I'll hunt you down and kill you. Kill you good. Kill your girlfriend too. I'll find your mother and father and brothers and sisters – anyone you have – and kill them too. I'll find your dog and your cat and gut them.*
>
> X: *I know.*
>
> MA: *If you know, then get the fuck out of my office right now. You're going to shoot me, Mr Smokin' Joe Policeman? In cold blood? In cold blood? Nah.*
>
> X2: *Wait. Don't shoot him. Doc? Doc? You'll never guess who*

we got on Ma's floor. Investigator Ng. What do we do? Come in.

Ng switched the cassette off. He looked at Doc who looked embarrassed. 'You stopped him from killing me. Why? Off the record.'

'Totally off the record?'

'Totally.'

Doc weighed his words. 'You were going to murder Ma. But he was mine. His death belonged to me.'

'You could have killed me anyway.'

'I figured the place was wired.'

'You're lying.'

'Yeah. Truth is – if possible, I don't want you dead.'

'Until next time.'

Doc grinned, conceding Ng's point. 'Until next time.'

Ng, more business: 'Have you got Ma?'

'Oh yeah.'

'Is he dead?'

'Oh yeah. He's sleeping with the sharks, but real big-time.'

Doc couldn't tell if Ng was pleased or indifferent.

'I saw his video. The girl,' said Ng.

'Yeah. Me too. I figure Ma's an innocent murder.'

'There are no innocent murders.'

'Sure there are. For instance, it always struck me as funny that the two Chinks – Ma's boys – who were shot in the park were the boys who did over your friend, the showbiz woman.'

'Leave her out of this.'

'Oh, I do, Mr Ng. And I will. (pause) The thing is . . . those Chinks – Ma's boys – they would have been hard to surprise. Don't you think? Hard to kill. Don't you think? What d'you think, Mr Ng?'

Ng took the tape out of the micro-cassette and put it on the table. 'This is the police surveillance tape of Ma's kidnapping.

194

It's the only copy. It's yours.'

He reached into his bag, took out a single photo and placed it next to the tape. Doc picked it up.

Eight cages.
In the foreground of one cage, a half-face with one eye open, looking puzzled.
A hand.
A half-foot.
A foot.
Eight cages of extra-meaty, double-crunchy shark food.
A sign on the boat's side: 'OC'S PRI'.

'This is the only copy of the photograph. It's yours.'

'Why you doing this, Ng?'

'Because you could have had me killed at Ma's and didn't.'

Mortaferi leant back in his chair. 'You're lying.'

Ng seemed not to have heard.

Doc: 'You're buying me. You're buying protection.'

Ng looked at Doc, then looked away.

'And you want me to think it's for you. But you're not buying protection for you. Are you? It's for her.'

Ng, softly: 'One warning. If she's ever hurt again, I'll blame you. Tell your friends.'

Doc nodded.

'All your friends.'

Doc nodded again. 'I understand.'

Ng moved to the door and opened it. Alfred got there too late.

Doc: 'Hey! The tape! The photo! Are these *really* the only copies?'

But Ng was gone. ✱

There was a car parked round the corner, D.C. Lilly behind the wheel.

'How did it go?' she said.

He refused to look her in the eye. 'Well, I think.'

She felt shame coming out of him as sorrow and heat. 'You've done the right thing, Ng. She's lucky to have you; and she's wrong.'

Ng shook his head. I don't want to talk about it.

'Ng. She's wrong.'

*

At Best Rest they shook hands goodbye.

EPILOGUE

Stella resisted the urge to phone Ng.

I'm a showbiz journo play-acting at being a detective. If it's going to cost blood, fuck it. Fuck him. Fuck em all.

She tried to bury herself in *The Pentangeli Papers*.

*

SHOWBIZ! SHOWBIZ! SHOWBIZ! ONLINE!
THE PENTANGELI PAPERS ***EXCLUSIVE***!
OH NO! THE EFFIES ARE HERE AGAIN!
F for Favourites, F for Fabulous, F for Fun, F is for Frowing Up.
Like its near-namesake, the Emmys, the Effies are a bore and a chore but Mother TVbiz likes to protect her offspring by wrapping them in emeralds, ermine and ego.
Mother TVbiz pretends the networks love them and their viewers and make only top-shelf programs for them.
How else to ape Hollywood here in this wide brown land?
How else to tell which of Mother's sons and daughters are stars? How . . .

*

For all their many faults, Mo Sherlock and Rex Clap were sentimentalists who truly loved showbiz. So Mo was more than willing to listen when Clap suggested that this years' Effies should 'contain a film tribute to the late great Frank String. Four or five minutes. What do you say, Mo?'

It helped to clarify their minds that (softly, softly) Clap could end Mo's career by leaking details about industrial espionage. But then again, Mo (softly, softly) could tell a waiting world about Sir Rex illegally taping workers in dressing rooms. Zwikky had told her all about it.

Best to call a truce.

'A tribute. Sir Rex, you're really just an old softie, aren't you?'

'Yes, Mo. Yes I am.'

'It's a FABULOUS idea.'

So Frank String – *'one of the truly great actors'* (Channel 4 Press Release) who *'died, literally, in the saddle, before the cameras, surrounded by his Channel 3 family'* (Channel 3 Press Release) – was to have one last strut and fret upon the stage.

*

Soon the days were a week and the week was a month and Stella thought she was starting to recover from Ng. Then, one night, as swiftly and savagely as an alcoholic's craving, she had to see him. No reason. Just had to.

She grabbed her car keys and headed out, her pitty-pat heart already thumping.

*

Stella had too much respect for Ng's police skills to park close to the shabby motel. Instead she parked in a laneway and walked there. She stood in deep shadows and spied. She remembered the last time this Ngian compulsion gripped her. Roaring drunk and determined to bed him, she'd driven to Best Rest, opened her mouth to declare herself then vomited on his shoes and passed out.

Happy times.

Ng's lights were on but nothing moved. At first she thought he must be asleep then a shadow moved inside and silhouetted on a blind. She'd always suspected he had trouble sleeping. Some days there had been bruises under his eyes and his face would stay pale till noon.

Go to sleep.

An hour passed. Two. A brief silhouette. Two. No more. She shivered in the shadow and air.

This is stupid.

She went home.

＊

Even Ng's courage didn't extend to picking up the phone to speak to Stella. Or, rather, he would pick up the phone, then put it down. He would pick it up, start to dial her number then put it down. Once he let it ring for half a tone, then slammed it down and his hand was trembling with adrenalin.

They had known from almost the beginning that each had coward hearts. Both knew that maybe their hearts were right to be cowards and that maybe they couldn't and shouldn't be together.

Ng stopped picking up the phone.

Stella stopped her night visits to the sad motel.

＊

Sir Rex's wife, Lady Roberta Clap, never went to the Effies, never went to TVbiz functions, and never went to Channel 3. She liked to pretend her husband's fortune came from inherited

wealth and that she had never been an A/M/W (Actress/
Model/Whatever) in her distant youth. On this night of
nights, instead of escorting the usual bimbette from *Balls*
or *The Homicide Boys*, Sir Rex hoped it would be Stella on
his arm.

*

Stella hated these tinhorn sham glam affairs, she feared
crowds and she would need several neat Beefeaters and a
TranQuax to even walk down the red carpet. So, when the
great man appealed to the better angels of Stella's nature,
she said –

'No way.'

Clap: 'Pentangeli. You must honour Frank's memory. It's
what he would have wanted.'

'Forget it.'

'Please Pentangeli.'

He's right. Shit.

*

The red carpet was lined 30-deep with fans who screamed
lusty approval as each long black limo deposited its precious
cargo.

'Ahh Kylie!'

'Ahh Russell!'

'AhhhEeeeee Brandywine!'

And this year's hunks and spunks and freeze-dried-smile
veterans got out and tottered down the red carpet, waving at
photogs and fans and thus the rite was fulfilled.

'Who's that?'

Stella and Sir Rex walked arm-in-arm down the carpet.
In keeping with his image, Rex wore the extra-steely glare
he reserved for such occasions. Stella wore tens of thousands

of dollars of jewels and gowns and looked *comme on dit*, 'radiant' and 'fabulous', her paper-white hair a welcome glimpse of exotica in a sea of blonde. Only Clap felt the trembly nervousness in her arms.

'Nearly there.'

Then they were inside the State Theatre Playhouse. Norman had stashed a large flask of Beefeater Gin under the programme. Stella palmed the flask and retired to the ladies' for a bracer. The VIP seats were always near the toilets for the drunks or otherwise bladder-impaired or the can't-quit-smoking rich. 'Sitters' – gowned and tuxedo-ed models hired for the night – waited along the walls to take their place lest the cameras see – Ahh! – an empty seat.

Stella spotted Zwikky a few rows behind but he ignored her.

*

The cameras rolled. The MC, 'Gra-Gra' – a bug-eyed show-biz favourite – said nada nada nada and people clapped and laughed and some shitty dancers performed some half-bright choreographer's vision of nada nada nada entertainment. Giddy dim people monologued endlessly. Nada Nada won for Best Supporting Actor and thanked 'everybody, especially you, Mum' and Nada Nadette won for Best Supporting Actress and thanked her dad.

TY&TN won for Best Drama for the third year in a row. Normally Elias Zwik would have been the man to accept the award but, even as Zwik rose, Sir Rex stood up and strode to the stage. Whispers ran around *tout le ballroom* –

'Zwikky's out.'

'Zwikky's out.'

'Zwikky's out.'

Sir Rex, in a very un-Clapian show of democratic senti-ment, spent his 90 seconds thanking 'the little people, the script girls, the grips, the unsung heroes of our great enterprise.' It went down a treat.

Then Gra-Gra introduced the tribute to Frank String and magic came into the evening for the first time. Snippets of his early UK career, his later Hollywood days, his much later camp-it-up Hollywood days, even a snippet of the ad for Youngman incontinence pads.

'God, he was so beautiful . . .'

'And so *funny*.'

'Even the *ad*'s good.'

*

Everyone agreed that Stella Pentangeli's on-line thing put it best.

KING FRANK

Frank String boasted that he had never let his public or his
director down, so it was fitting that he kept death
waiting till he finished his last scene.
Just as fitting was the tribute payed him tonight.
Footage of his months in TY&TN hushed the crowd who saw
for the first time just how good String was.
Harold Bellbird, as created by String, was a comical-tragic
creation who lived and breathed whole – even as fate threw
whatever the writers came up with at him and his clan.
Harold Bellbird was a man in love with life and twice as big.
He had what only the best have – whether onstage or on the big
screen or even in humble little soaps – he had true-ness.
And when dying Harold said, 'Life is hard, Brooke. But, O, it's
so good. So very, very good,' and his soul went riding towards
the mountain – his mountain – we went with him.
His fall to the ground was our fall and Brooke's grief was ours.
String brought a bit of class to a business that so seldom has

*any; and – who would have thought it? – tonight he
brought a bit of class even to the effin' Effies.*

*

Frank got a standing ovation which took two precious TV
minutes for Gra-Gra to calm. Just as the tears were drying,
Gra-Gra announced that the winner of the Gold Effie, TV's
Holy Grail, was the late Frank String. The crowd got to its
feet, roaring, clapping, louder and louder and no order was
possible.

That's a wrap, Frank.

*

Ned Puccini senses that Mr Ning is sad. Ned makes it
his business, for the first time ever, to sit in Room 11 with
Mr Ning as he watches the TV which Mr Ning never
watches usually. It's the Effies. Ned loves the Effies. He likes
the way everyone is beautiful and nice and loves each other.
Ned tries to remember to make himself concentrate on
Mr Ning, too, and not just on the TV. It's hard but he does.
To his delight, the TV shows Mr Ning's lady friend, Stella,
who looks like a princess or even a queen tonight. Ned
says, 'Look. It's your lady friend,' but Mr Ning doesn't answer.
His friend comes on again. Then again. And every time
Mr Ning sees her, he looks away. This confuses Ned and
makes him sad.

He will try to remember to ask Mamma about it.

Also by Wakefield Press

MURDER BY MANUSCRIPT

Steve J. Spears

'Steve J. Spears storms the crime novel and makes it quiveringly, submissively, riotously his own.'

Bob Ellis

'A fast-paced, deliciously wicked parody of the world of showbiz. It has everything you could ever want from comic crime fiction – sex, drugs, laughs and a ridiculously high body count.'

Age Pick of the Week

All internationally renowned 'lady showbiz detective' Stella Pentangeli wants is to solve a simple literary riddle: did William Shakespeare belong to a blood-thirsty seventeenth-century cult which resurrected dead people?

All enigmatic and brilliant Investigator Ng wants is to find out why a relentless monster is using Shakespeare's personal recipe to make 'resurrection soup' out of twenty-first-century citizens.

As the body count mounts, all the serial killer wants is to add Stella and Ng to the menu.

For more information visit www.wakefieldpress.com.au

Also by Wakefield Press

THE TROJAN DOG

Dorothy Johnston

'Johnston achieves the difficult double feat: she creates and maintains a convincing physical world, and yet transcends it through a lovely and original imagination.'

Helen Garner

'I should ask your department's accountant whether he's missing nine hundred thousand bucks.' This is the anonymous message that will change Sandra Mahoney's life.

When a powerful but unpopular bureaucrat is accused of theft and computer fraud, Sandra is convinced that the charge is false. But how to track down the culprit when almost anyone could be an enemy? In her search for the truth, Sandra finds herself in a battle of wits against an elusive and unscrupulous opponent, a battle in which no one's allegiance can be taken for granted.

The Trojan Dog is a compelling story of computer crime, loyalty and betrayal against the backdrop of a city – and a country – on the cusp of political change.

Dorothy Johnston's novels have twice been short-listed for the Miles Franklin Award.

For more information visit www.wakefieldpress.com.au

Also by Wakefield Press

THE WHITE TOWER

Dorothy Johnston

'Here is the big major talent that publishers tell us no longer exists. If you combined the two strands of Ruth Rendell and her alter writing ego, Barbara Vine, you'd come close to Dorothy Johnston's talent.'

Ken Bruen

'Jumpers,' McCallum was saying. 'Jumpers are – well, in my experience jumpers are always badly disturbed. They choose to jump because it's so violent.'

A mild young man's addiction to a role-playing internet game has led to his death. Disturbingly, his suicide is a bizarre echo of his chilling execution in the game; his only note a digital mirror image of his own death.

But where do blame and responsibility lie, in a world where powerful men are as seductive as they are unscrupulous? Sandra Mahoney finds that the threads of truth and illusion can easily wind into a choking scarf of manipulation and deceit.

For more information visit www.wakefieldpress.com.au

Wakefield Press is an independent publishing and
distribution company based in Adelaide, South Australia.
We love good stories and publish beautiful books.
To see our full range of titles, please visit our website at
www.wakefieldpress.com.au.

Wakefield Press thanks Fox Creek Wines
and Arts South Australia for their support.